THE GANYMEDE TAKEOVER

✳

The three guerillas made a raid for food and supplies. The defenders kept them off with lasers. So they used the strange new weapons that they had found. The illusion machines. They worked well. Twenty-four phantom men who fought like veterans helped to carry the captured supplies up into the mountains.

Later they conjured up a complete army of illusions: giant vampires, man-eating plants, Valkyries, cannibal children.

The trouble was, when they switched off the machines: the phantoms didn't go away....

Philip K. Dick and Ray Nelson

The Ganymede Takeover

ARROW BOOKS

ARROW BOOKS LTD
3 Fitzroy Square, London W1

AN IMPRINT OF THE HUTCHINSON GROUP

London Melbourne Sydney Auckland
Wellington Johannesburg Cape Town
and agencies throughout the world

First published by
Ace Books Inc. 1967
Arrow edition 1971

*Made and printed in Great Britain
by The Anchor Press Ltd.,
Tiptree, Essex*
ISBN 0 09 005370 2

for Kirsten and Nancy

At three in the morning the vidphone rang on the bedtable of Rudolph Balkani, Chief of the Bureau of Psychedelic Research. It rang for a long time before Balkani answered it, though—as so often of late—he had been awake for hours.

'Yes, this is Balkani.'

'I want some information,' a worried voice on the other end of the line said. Balkani recognised the voice of the Chairman of the United Nations Security Council. 'I thought we could have a little talk. . . .'

'Make it brief,' Balkani said. 'I'm a sick man.'

'Did you hear the 'cast?'

'What 'cast?' He scratched his bearded chin.

'The alien ultimatum. It came over all the TV and radio—'

'I don't waste my time with the mass entertainment media,' Balkani said. 'What did they have to offer?'

' "We bring you peace. We bring you unity." '

'Spare me the propaganda. I gather they demand the unconditional surrender of Earth.'

'That's right. But aren't you involved in developing some sort of new mind-gadget, Doctor? Won't that stop them?'

'True,' Balkani said with a touch of irony. 'But unfortunately it will also stop us. It will, in fact, stop everything on or around this planet which happens to possess a mind.'

'I understood you could render some people immune to it. Say, vital first-line leaders.'

'Not yet. The only defence against it would be the radical psychotherapy I'm working with. If you'd give me a little time and an ample supply of, shall we say, "volunteers" for my experiments . . .'

'We've got to have it now!' the Chairman of the Security Council grated. With visible effort he got control of himself; on the vidscreen his image became fixedly tranquil. 'What do you advise?'

'I don't advise,' Balkani said. 'I'm just the witch doctor in this tribe, not the chief. I make the little voodoo dolls, but it's your job to decide whether or not to stick pins into them. However, I do have one favour to ask of you.'

'What is that?'

'If you decide to use the thing, don't tell me. I don't want to know.' Having said that Balkani hung up, rolled over and continued trying to sleep.

'Too unspecialised,' Mekkis muttered, eyeing the captive human with distaste. 'However, with a little selective breeding . . .'

The Timekeeper fluttered near Mekkis' ear and said softly. 'Better start to ready yourself for the meeting of the Grand Council.'

'Yes, yes, of course,' Mekkis said. His long, slender tongue whipped out and touched a pushbutton next to his couch. At once his dressers came scampering in, twittering excitedly to each other. Mekkis hunched himself up to make the task easier for them.

He was, like all members of the Ganymedian ruling species, legless, armless, pink and very much like a large worm in appearance. He did not need arms and legs of his own. The creeches constituted his arms and legs; this summed up their purpose in existing. It was for that they had been born, were bred.

Now they busily slipped him into his finest red-orange formal sack. Nothing but the best for what might well be the most important day of his career in government service. Tiny grooms skittered over his head and set to work combing his extensive lashes, while washers, with their tongues, attended his cheeks. During this he glanced once more at the captive human. *Poor creatures,* he thought. *You should never have called our attention to your presence in the system.*

Mekkis had personally argued against the war. But— now it had been accomplished. 'Too late for tears,' he murmured aloud. 'And it isn't so bad being a creech. Is it, my friends?'

'No, no, it's all right,' twittered the infinitely varied crowd of specialised beings that had gathered around him, making him ready.

'First conquer, then occupy, then absorb. That's the way it's done. We've already gotten past the initial two phases without too much difficulty . . . unless I'm wildly mistaken, today we pass into phase three.' *And*, he thought, *that's where I come in.*

To make absolutely certain he called for his Oracle. Serpent-like the Oracle approached.

'What say you for the future?' Mekkis demanded.

'For today?' the precog said. Mekkis noticed with uneasiness that the creech seemed unwilling to prophesy.

'Yes, out with it!'

'The powers of darkness gather for you. It is the day of your enemies!'

Mekkis licked his lips and said, 'But after that?'

'More darkness, and greater darkness, and finally, oh my good master, darkness for us all!'

Mekkis pondered this soberly. The Oracle had advised against the invasion of Earth; hence Mekkis' own opposition. But the invasion had been a success. There were those who doubted the power of Oracles. *Perhaps,* he conjectured, *the future is unknowable after all. It's easy enough to utter vague and frightening words that nobody really understands, then later on say, 'You see? That's what I meant all along.'*

'These powers of darkness,' Mekkis said aloud. 'Is there anything I can do to evade them?'

'Today? Nothing. But after that—a slim chance. If you solve the riddle of the Nowhere Girl.'

'What Nowhere Girl?' Mekkis retained his composure only with great effort.

'My faculty is limited and my vision is fading. But I see something approaching from the future which I find no words to describe. It has the manner of a vast cavity that reaches out to draw us in! Already it is so powerful that it bends the stream of time. The closer you get to it the harder it will be to evade it. Oh master, I'm afraid! I, who have never been afraid before, am now eclipsed by terror.'

Mekkis thought, *There's nothing I can do to evade my misfortune today, so I might as well go forth and meet it, without flinching or blanching. I can't control the fates, but I can control my reaction to them.*

With a wave of his tongue he summoned his carriers and started for the Hall of the Grand Council.

On the wall of the Grand Council Hall hung a great clock. All those who belonged to what one might call the Progressive Faction sat on the same side of the chamber as the clock. It was the clock faction that had pushed through the war against Earth. Those who sat on the side away from the clock comprised what one might call the Conservatives. They had, unsuccessfully, opposed the war. It was to this faction that Mekkis belonged.

When Mekkis manifested himself in the hall with customary pomp he discovered no one reposing on the anti-clock side. Everyone, in entering, had gathered about the clock leaders; Mekkis, lowered to the thick carpet by his carriers, remained inert, stunned.

But he had already sworn a moral oath to himself. Painfully and steadily he made his way toward his traditional tooth-carved niche on the anti-clock side; there, alone, he took up the formal bent posture and eyed the senile idiots of the bench. And recalled, as he waited, that the expected darkness lay for him at tongue's end.

They won the war, he thought to himself, *and that gives them the fulcrum to pry the dribbling Electors into ratifying all their future connivances. I, however, will never give in. But—I will not be the order-giver. Only order-carry-outer.*

Seeing him present the Electors at the bench convened this most important session.

'In your absence,' came the thought from the Mind Group, 'we initiated the distribution of Terran rulership. Your area awaits you, naturally; you have not been ignored.'

Mekkis retorted with huge irony, 'And what bale is left for me?' No doubt a worthless scrap of a bale, the dregs. He experienced through the union of the Group Mind the collective sardonic amusement of the Common, directed at him; they enjoyed his frustration and impotence. 'Name me that bale,' he said, and prepared to endure it, whatever it consisted of, however ignoble.

'The bale,' the Chief Elector informed him gleefully, 'arranged for your management, is the Bale of Tennessee.'

'Allow me to consult my reference material,' Mekkis said, and, by telepathic communication, established contact with his librarian at his residence. A moment later there visually appeared within his brain a full description, itemisation and map of the bale. And evaluation thereof.

Mekkis fainted dead away.

The next he knew he lay supine in the general chamber of Major Cardinal Zency's residence; he had been transported to the home of his friend to recover his wits.

'We tried to prepare you,' Zency said, coiled nearby solicitously. 'A little splash of brigwater and laut? It'll clear your head.'

'The pnagdruls,' Mekkis swore thickly.

'Well, you'll live many more years. Eventually . . .'

'A lifetime of work.' He managed to raise the foreportion of his body and steady himself. 'I won't go. I'll resign from public service.'

'Then you can never again . . .'

'I don't *want* ever again to enter the Common. I'll live out my life on a satellite. Alone.' He felt rotten. As if he had been stepped on by one of the clumsy enormous bipedal lower life forms. 'Please. Give me something to lap.'

Presently an obliging staff member of Zency's domicile placed an ornate, chaste dish before him; he lapped dully, blindly, as Zency watched with concern.

'There are,' he said presently, 'unpacified Negroes in that bale. And hordes of Chipua and Chawkta

Indians holed up there in the mountains. It's the bung-hole of the conquered realms. And they know it; that's why they gave it to me. It's deliberate!' He hissed with wrath, totally ineffectual wrath. 'More brigwater.' He beckoned to a miserably inferior species of household servant. It approached.

'Perhaps,' Major Cardinal Zency said tactfully, 'it's a compliment. The one bale which requires genuine work . . . the sole area our military failed to neutralise. Now they've given up, turned it over to you. No one else wants to handle it; it's too tough.'

At that Mekkis stirred. The idea, although it smacked of self-serving rationalisation, roused him slightly. Had he thought of it himself he would have been forced on ethical grounds to dismiss it. But Zency, whom he respected, had advanced it; that took the onus from it. But even so he did not want the task. If the military had failed, how could he succeed? Distortedly he recalled news reports about the Neeg partisans in the mountains of Tennessee, their fanatical and skilful leader, Percy X, who had eluded all the homotropic destruct devices programmed with him in mind. He could imagine himself confronted by Percy X, in addition to the demand from the Council that, as in all other bales, he carry out the customary programme: destroy the local structure of government and create an overall puppet monarch.

'Tell them,' he said to the Major Cardinal, 'that I'm sick; I swallowed too large a gork egg and it's stuck along my digestive tract somewhere. I'll be lucky if I don't burst—you know, the way Cpogrb did last year when he consumed—what was it?—four gork eggs at a single sitting. What a sight; pieces of him turned up all over the dining room.' Memory warmed him momentarily, memory of a fine Common-mind get-together, a

13

fusion for gaiety and pleasure without the compulsion of duty emanating from the core of the polyencephalic mind, the Electors of the Bench and the powerful entities of the clock side of the hall.

'Look at it this way,' the Major Cardinal said. 'If you succeed you'll make your military predecessor look like a fool—will make the whole military faction look like fools, in fact.'

'That's true,' Mekkis said slowly. A plan had found its way into his mind. Tennessee was at present a hodge-podge of more or less autonomous feudal entities, each centred on some plantation owner or merchant prince, a condition which had resulted from the collapse of Earth's central government. It would be Mekkis' task to select one of these tiny tyrants and elevate him to sovereignty over the entire bale, above all his jealous compeers. No easy task that; no matter whom he picked there would be objections, even hatred, from the others. *But what if he picked Percy X?* Who else would be more grateful for the authority and thus more docile a puppet? Naturally the merchant princes would cluck frantically, but they would no matter who was chosen; this way perhaps the Neegs and Indians could be pacified and the rulership decided all in one swift act.

'That's true,' Mekkis said again, this time with a note of hope in his voice. There was no longer any question of backing out.

Certainly the prophet on his staff had been right; there had lain something to be wary of directly in his path today. And he had squirmed directly into it, head-on. As usual.

And, as usual, he saw a solution—to his advantage.

The hotel room, second-rate, dirty and dilapidated as it was, managed to cackle in a senile but penetrating voice, 'Mr Paying Guest, do not attempt to leave without settling your bill at the desk downstairs.'

Anyhow, Joan Hiashi reflected, *it doesn't have an artificial Southern accent built into its circuit, even down this far in Swenesgard, Tennessee.* 'I was,' she said with a toss of her head, 'merely looking out the window. You don't keep yourself too clean, do you?'

'At the miniscule rates charged for me . . .'

Well, that certainly was true. And the hotel still accepted the old UN currency, recalled by the occupation authorities throughout most of the planet. But news of the mandatory currency-redemption evidently hadn't reached the bale of Tennessee. And that was good, because about all she had brought with her was the familiar, now wrinkled and worn UN bills, plus her pre-war credit cards, a whole pack of them, for whatever they might be worth here.

And, in addition, her head hurt. The fresh air from outside did nothing to help it; in fact, if anything the air made it worse because it was the stale and flaccid wind of an unfamiliar, inconsiderate foreign area. She had never been in the bale of Tennessee before but she knew how, during the war, it had unglued itself from the national identity, decaying into a self-contained and dreary little state cryptic to Northerners such as herself. And yet, because of her business, she had to be here.

To the autonomic articulation circuit of the hotel room—feeble, of some crude pre-war design—she said,

'What can you tell me about the local ethnic folk singers?'

'What's that, Mr Paying Guest? Repeat your query.'

She had already told it several times that she was a 'Miss', not a 'Mister', but it was, it seemed, programmed to use only one form of address. Firmly, she said, 'This area, the south in general has for a century and a half produced the finest native jazz and ballad singers in the entire country. Buell Kazee, for instance, came from Grinder's Switch, not far from here. Bascom Lamar Lunsford, the greatest of them all, came from South Turkey Creek, North Carolina. Uncle Dave Macon . . .'

'A dime.'

'What?'

'If you're going to interrogate or pontificate you just insert a UN silver dime in the appropriate slot mounted handily at eye-level slightly to your left.'

Joan Hiashi said, 'You don't recognise any of the names, do you?'

Reluctantly the seedy, deteriorating hotel room admitted, 'No.'

'One of the first true jazz recordings,' Joan said, sitting down on the crooked, narrow bed and opening her purse, 'was grooved by the Brunswick Company in 1927. The Reverend Edward Clayburn singing *True Religion*. That was one hundred and twenty years ago.' She took out a pack of Nirvana filter-tip marihuana cigarettes and lit one. They were not the best, but since they were manufactured by the company for which she worked she got them free. 'I know,' she continued, after a pause for holding the smoke deep in her lungs, 'that other more recent—I mean currently active sources— are alive here in this backwater, cut-off, boondock bale.

16

I intend to find them and video tape them for my TV show.'

The hotel room said, 'I am dealing, then, with a personality?'

'You might say that. I have an audience of twenty million. And the Bureau of Cultural Control has honoured me with an award for the best musical series of the year.'

'Then,' the hotel room said sagely, 'you can afford a dime.'

She paid the mechanism its dime.

'As a matter of fact,' the hotel room said, spurred into life by the coin, 'I have at an earlier occasion composed a ballad of my own. I sing in the style of Doc Boggs. The ballad is called . . .'

'Hotel rooms,' Joan said, 'even run-down ones, are not ethnic.'

She could have sworn she heard the old hotel room sigh. It was strange. But in fact these machines had become old and worn out, had begun making mistakes; therefore they began to seem almost human. In irritation she punched at its *off* stud and the garrulous construct wheezed into inactivity. Leaving her, mercifully, to plan her next step.

The Tennessee hills—controlled by the feral and un-co-operative bands of Neeg-parts; if they wouldn't do business with the Burgers and the plantations nor with the Ganymedian occupation authority, on what basis could she approach them? Through her reputation? Even the broken and corroding old hotel room, built probably back in '99, had wanted to get into the act. It was reasonable, then, to suppose that Percy X, too, would like to reach a larger audience. Everyone, after all, had an ego.

17

It was too bad, she reflected, that she couldn't paint herself coffee-colour, call herself a Neeg and temporarily, for her own purposes, join them—not as a prying white potentially hostile visitor but as a new recruit.

She eyed herself critically in the cracked and yellowed mirror.

The Japanese blood was rather dilute, unfortunately. It gave her chitin-like black hair and eyes to match and a small, delicate body . . . but very little else. Perhaps she could pass for an Indian. There were Indians among the Neeg-parts, she had heard. *But no,* she thought sadly; *there's no use kidding myself: I'm white. And white, to these descendants of the cult of Black Muslims, is white. I'll just have to play it by ear,* she decided.

From her luggage she took a pair of clinging but warm powder blue nylon coveralls. Sexy but tasteful, and in the latest fashion. She had observed some of the clothing worn by women in this out-of-the-way bale, but even for the sake of protective coloration she could not bring herself to wear such museum pieces. It seemed that the unisexual mode, standard for at least fifty years in the outside world, had not as yet penetrated to Tennessee. This might well be the only spot left in the world where women's clothing differed from men's.

At the aud-phone dangling by only a few of its screws from the wall of the room she dialled the code number of the local taxi service. And then sat waiting, with her recording gear piled beside her, for the ionocraft cab to appear.

I'm still thinking, Paul Rivers told himself early that morning. He then heaved a wistful sigh and rolled over to give his belly the same opportunity to acquire a sunburn as his back had had. *Here I lie, surrounded by the*

18

silent flesh of my fellow human beings, he said to himself
with a trace of bitterness, *and my mind goes nattering
on, as if I were back at the university lecturing to some
slightly dense class of undergraduates. My body is here
but my mind—perhaps, students, the central problem of
man is that he is never where he is, but always where he
is going or where he has come from. Thus, when I am
alone I am not really alone. And when I am with someone I am not really with them.*

How, he asked himself almost angrily, *do I get my
mind to shut its big energetic mouth?*

While lying face up Paul Rivers had kept his eyes
closed to protect himself against the brightness of the
sun, seeing nothing but the redness of that light, it being
still uncomfortably bright as it filtered through his eye-
lids in lurid, vague, oozing patterns. Now, his face turned
away from the sun, he felt safe in opening his eyes.

The first sight that greeted his disgusted vision consisted of an empty tranquilliser bottle half-buried in the
sand. Smell of salt-sea breeze, too; refreshing tang in the
aroma of putrid seaweed and expired fish. Listen: the
breathing rush of waves, endless birth, growth and death
that means nothing. Distant shouts and laughter of the
supposedly enlightened and innocent, but actually
groggy and drugged; this done by the lethal occupying
authority. *Taste while you can,* he commanded himself,
*that healthy sand in your mouth; feel it crunch and grind
in your teeth. Experience that delightful tickle of sand
fleas walking on your baking backside! This,* he told
himself sternly, *is real living.*

He was, however, unable to prevent himself from
reading, instead, the lable on the bottle. *I am,* he had to
admit, *my own most hopeless case.*

A shadow fell upon the still-life of the tranquilliser

bottle in the nearby sand and Paul Rivers glanced up. Slowly. He couldn't place the face; the nipples, however, were familiar. Ah, he now remembered. It was Miss Holly Something-or-Other, the Vice-President of the local chapter of the Sexual Freedom Society. Perhaps in order to avoid the appearance of complete nudity she wore a pair of horn-rimmed, oval-lensed sunglasses. *She must be in her late teens or early twenties,* he thought vaguely. *A little too young for me, possibly, but still . . .*

Tall and tawny, with Earth-mother brown hair falling loosely to the small of her back, Miss Holly stood over him with a gentle smile on her full, unlipsticked lips and met his gaze with half-closed, fearless eyes. Miss Holly was, he decided, the only good argument he had yet come across for the principles of the Sexual Freedom Society but she was, simply in being as she was, a very persuasive, if not conclusive, one. Without a word she knelt, leaned over and kissed him lightly on the cheek.

Her gesture of greeting completed, she wet her lips with her tongue and spoke. 'Vidphone call for you, Doctor Rivers.' He noticed for the first time that she was holding in her palm a cigarette-package-sized vidphone. *How can this be?* he thought. *Nobody but the central office knows where I am, and they wouldn't bother me on my vacation.* Puzzled, he took the vidphone and focused his eyes on the tiny screen. It was, indeed, the home office; he recognised the image as his immediate superior, Dr Martin Choate. Because of the 3-D and colour Dr Choate looked like some sort of underworld elf peering up out of an imprisoning box.

'Hello, elf,' Paul Rivers said.

'How's that?' Dr Choate said, mildly startled. 'Now,

Rivers, you know I wouldn't disturb you if it wasn't important.'

'Yes?' Paul Rivers said patiently, in the encouraging voice he had developed from long practice in getting reluctant talkers to come to the point.

'I have a patient for you,' Dr Choate said, and stopped again, searching for words.

'Who is it?'

Dr Choate cleared his throat, smiled weakly and said, 'The human race.'

Dingy, with scaling enamel, once bright green but now the colour of mould, the tattered ionocraft taxi settled into the locking frame at the window of Joan Hiashi's elderly hotel room. 'Make it snappy,' it said officiously, as if it had urgent business in this collapsing environment, this meagre plantation of a state once a portion of a great national union. 'My meter,' it added, 'is already on.' The thing, in its inadequate way, was making a routine attempt to intimidate her. And she did not enjoy that.

'Help me load my gear,' Joan answered it.

Swiftly—astonishingly so—the ionocraft shot a manual tensor through the open window, grappled the recording gear, transferred the units to its storage compartment. Joan Hiashi then boarded it.

As she made her exit the door to the hotel room opened. A thick-necked, paunchy, middle-aged man, smoking a yellowish cigar, appeared. And said, 'I'm Gus Swenesgard; I'm the owner of this plantation and I own this hotel and this room says you're trying to escape without paying.' His tone was neutral, as if it neither angered nor surprised him.

'You will notice,' Joan said wearily, 'that I am leaving behind all my clothes except for what I have on. I'm here on a business trip; I'll be back in a day or so.' It astonished her that a Burger, the feudal baron of the whole plantation area which included this town of Swenesgard, would take a personal interest in such a small matter.

As if reading her mind—and perhaps he was; perhaps Gus Swenesgard was a telepath trained by the Bureau of Psychedelic Research—the sweat-stained, big-footed Burger said, 'I keep tabs on everything, Miss Hiashi. Like, I mean, you're the only important, famous-type guest the Olympus Arms has had in months, and you're not creeping out like a . . .' He gestured with the cigar. 'A worm. On your belly, if you'll pardon my saying so.'

'Pretty small plantation you've got here,' Joan observed, 'if you can afford to do that.' She got out a handful of UN bills. 'If it distresses your neurotic mind I'll pay in advance. For six days. I'm surprised they didn't ask for it at the desk when I registered.'

'Aw,' Gus Swenesgard said, accepting the bills and counting them, 'we trust you.'

'I can see that.' She wanted to get on her way; what did this old idiot have in mind, really?

'Come on, miss. We know you're a Neeg-lover.' The man reached out and gave her an overly familiar pat on the head. 'We've watched your shows, my family and me. Always a lot of Neegs on it, aren't there? Even my six-year-old, Eddie; he said it. "That lady's a Neeg-lover." I'll just bet you're on your way up to the hills to visit Percy X. Isn't that right, miss?'

After a pause Joan said, 'Yes.'

'Now I'll tell you what.' Gus Swenesgard pocketed the bills; they bulged, wadded-up, in his uncreased

22

trousers pocket. The pants had to be at least ten years old; nobody made clothes with pockets in them any more. 'You may be a Neeg-lover but that don't mean they feel the same about you. Those 'parts, they're insane. Like African savages. They'll mutilate you.' He nodded his red near-bald head emphatically, with great earnestness. 'Up in the North you don't realise that; all your Neegs have missed.'

' "Missed"?' She did not know the term; it was obviously one of local use, and perjorative.

'Miscegenated. You know; mixed their blood in with you whites so you're all contaminated. But down here it's different; we know how to treat our Toms; we know where they belong.'

'For their own good?' Joan said caustically.

'They're happy. They got security. They don't have to worry about being commandeered for any Gany work camps.'

Uneasily, Joan said, 'I didn't know that the conquerors had work camps.'

'They didn't take over this planet for nothing, miss. They haven't begun to requisition labour crews yet. But they will. They'll take 'em back to Ganymede and make them into what they call "creeches". I got inside dope on it. But we mean to protect our Toms; they've worked for us good and we owe that to them.' Gus Swenesgard's voice was unwavering, tough with harshness.

'It's pointless, Mister Swenesgard,' came a soft but professionally commanding voice from behind the two of them. Gus turned rapidly, startled, to face the newcomer. So did Joan.

'What . . . ?' began Gus.

'She has her mind made up,' the stranger continued quietly. 'If you are really so interested in Miss Hiashi's welfare, it seems to me that the only thing you can do is offer to go along with her. To protect her.'

'I don't know who you are or think you are,' Gus said emphatically, 'but you, mister, are out of your mind.'

'My name is Paul Rivers.' He extended his hand and Gus, with reluctance, shook it. 'I sense you're afraid, sir.'

'Any man with an ounce of intelligence would be,' Gus snapped. 'Those Neegs . . .'

'The Greeks believed, in their more philosophical moments,' Paul Rivers said, 'that there was only one blessing greater than a short life, and that was never to have been born at all. In times like these, one can see a great deal of wisdom in this.'

'If you're so damn philosophical,' Gus said angrily, 'you go with her.'

Turning to Joan, Paul Rivers said, 'If you'll allow me.'

Joan looked at him and felt suspicion. Lean, probably in his late thirties, with touches of grey in his close-cropped, well-groomed black hair, he seemed so calm, so self-confident; he seemed, in fact, perfectly sincere, and yet it struck her as incredible that someone would put his life in jeopardy for nothing, no matter how philosophical he might be. Still . . .

'All right,' Joan decided. 'If you're nutty enough to come I'm nutty enough to let you.' *No use questioning him,* she thought. *He could probably lie himself blue and I'd never know it.*

'If you'll wait a moment,' Paul Rivers said, moving towards the door, 'I'll go to my room and get a needle gun.' He departed.

And the moment he left the room she changed her

mind—violently. The air of confidence which Rivers possessed could only come from one thing. Obviously, he never expected to arrive at the point, the place where danger would threaten him. She thought, *Rivers must be someone hired to stop me from reaching Percy. Perhaps to kill me.*

'Can I leave now?' she asked Gus. 'My taxi says its meter is on.' Without waiting for an answer she crossed lightly through the open window and into the ionocraft.

'That Percy X,' Gus Swenesgard called after her, 'is a psychopath, descended from psychopaths, back to the first Black Muslims. You think to him you're going to be cute little Joan Hiashi, the TV darling? You'll be'— he followed to the window, gesturing with his cigar agitatedly as the taxi door shut—'one of those whites who lynched civil rights demonstrators back in 1966. You weren't even born then, but what's that matter to a fanatic like Percy X? I ask you; what's that mean to him —and how many yards of video tape you think you're going to groove before he . . .'

As the taxi door shut Joan shouted, 'Percy X and I went to college together. Comparative Religion One and Two at the Pacific School of Religion in Berkeley, California. We intended to be preachers, Mister Swenesgard. Isn't that crazy?' She gave the pedal sign to the cab and it uncoupled from the window.

Joan could not hear what Gus shouted after her in answer to that. The whoosh of the ionocraft climbing swiftly towards the sun drowned it out. *Strange,* she thought, *that Percy and I are going to meet again under such changed conditions. I've been studying Buddhism and he the religion of Mohammed, but somehow, during all the excitement, we have both gone a long way from where we had intended to go.*

25

'He doesn't want you to go,' the cab said sourly. 'But I don't care. If he revokes my licence I'll just switch over to another plantation. Like Chuck Pepitone's. It's big there; I'll bet I'd do six times the business.'

'Business is business,' Joan said, and settled back against the sagging imitation sea otter pelt seat.

'I'll say one thing for him,' the cab said. 'He does take an interest in what's going on around him. Most of the Burgers are too lofty to do anything but sip bourbon sours and ride horses. Gus, though; he takes the trouble to get me vital parts, hard-to-get parts. I'm sort of out of date, you know, and parts for me aren't easy to come by. And I always felt he sort of liked me.'

'He likes me, too,' Joan said, 'in his own knee-patting way. But I'm not turning back now, just to please him.' *Nor that other man who showed up,* she said to herself. *That Paul Rivers.*

In his hotel room Paul Rivers spoke hurriedly into his scrambler-equipped pocket vidphone. 'I've made contact with Joan Hiashi and she has agreed to let me accompany her into the mountains.'

'Good,' Dr Choate said. 'Now as you know, her analyst in New York has informed us that she is a collaborator out to supply the Gany Military with information leading to Percy's capture. As I explained in your briefing, this is something which we, of the World Psychiatric Association, cannot permit. Percy is a symbol for the human race now, an important ego-identification figure. As long as he continues to resist, so will the mass ego of humanity. Thus, it is vitally important that he continue, or at least seem to continue.'

'What if he doesn't?' Paul Rivers asked.

'The latest psycho-computer findings indicate that

26

this would lead to a massive increase in schizophrenia throughout the world, a thorough group insanity impossible to control. However there is one way to avoid this.'

'How?' Paul Rivers asked. He checked over his needle gun expertly and carefully as he spoke.

'Martyrdom. If he must die, it has to be a hero's death. The worms know this as well as we do. Our therapists attached to the office of Military Administrator Koli reports that Koli plans to capture Percy alive and have him skinned. The humiliation to the human ego were Percy to be skinned like a mere animal, for some sort of wall hanging, would constitute a traumatic incident of a magnitude difficult to overestimate. This, above all else, must not be allowed to happen.'

'Hmm,' Paul Rivers said, pocketing his needle gun.

'It's up to you, Rivers.' Choate then rang off; the miniature screen faded into an odd little slot of darkness.

Retracing his steps back down the hotel corridor, Paul Rivers reached Joan Hiashi's room; he pushed open the door and stepped inside.

Only Gus stood there. By the window, smiling. The smile alone told Paul Rivers an additional unpleasant fact.

'Mister Swenesgard,' he said in a low, level voice, *'you really wanted her to go.* Didn't you?'

The smile on the fat man's broad, moon-like face increased. 'Why, how you talk,' Gus said. 'And,' he added with satisfaction, 'there ain't no use trying to chase after her. That broken-down old ionocraft taxi she's in is the only one available.'

3

Lincoln Shaw sat sprawled in the hot sun with his back against a tree, frowningly repairing, for the hundredth time, the frame on his horn-rimmed glasses. He was a thin, small-boned mulatto with an air of cultured delicacy considerably out of place here in this mountain setting.

'Hey Lincoln,' came a shout from the other side of the clearing. 'Who that who freed the slaves?'

'I did,' Lincoln said automatically. This was a standing joke between Lincoln and Percy; he had long since ceased getting angry about it.

'No,' Percy roared, 'I did!'

'Nobody freed the slaves,' Lincoln muttered under his breath as Percy strode into the clearing carrying rabbits fresh from the traps.

'I heard that.' Percy threw himself down on the grass. 'And for once you're right. Nobody can free someone else; each man has got to do that for himself, right?'

'You make it sound so easy,' Lincoln said, brushing away one of the ubiquitous flies.

'Sure it's easy. Any man can have freedom if he's willing to die for it.'

'You mean kill for it,' Lincoln said absently.

'Right again.' Percy punched him on the arm.

'Damn it, man—that hurt. You always got to act like a goddam clown?'

'How do you want me to act?'

'With a little dignity. You're the leader of a major political movement; how can you expect anybody to respect you or what you stand for if you always act like a goddam clown?'

'You think maybe I ought to carry a ceremonial sword?' Percy said, amused.

'You'd stick yourself in the rear with it.' Lincoln glanced up briefly, blinked nearsightedly, then returned to fiddling with his glasses. 'But I'll tell you one thing for sure,' he added. 'If you act like dirt, people will treat you like dirt.'

Percy's hand shot out and clamped viciously onto Lincoln's wrist. 'Listen, man. You see the colour of my skin? It's dirt-colour. I'm dirt and so are you and so is everybody else in this so-called "political movement", and if you were a farmer instead of an egghead Northern intellectual you'd know that the best dirt is the blackest dirt. You're dirt, man, and don't forget it.'

'Yas*suh*, massuh boss,' Lincoln said, his usual overly-perfect English giving way to a whining parody of Good Old Uncle Tom. Percy laughed and released his grip.

'As a clown you got me beat from the word go,' Percy chuckled, but Lincoln only shrugged and returned to his work.

Alone in his office the worm Marshal Koli ruminated languidly in a torpor of wish-fulfilment fantasy as to the successful capture of Percy X. One final coup before he returned to Ganymede; before, mandatorily, he relinquished his post.

Peculiar that here on Terra the dark races held the lowest caste; it was obvious to every Ganymedian that the order was inverted from its natural hierarchy. After all, the Negroes presented a pleasing appearance and were endowed with—by and large—a natural, balanced philosophy of life, a moderation and subtle humour.

Whereas the Whites tended to hang frantically on the twin horns of ambition and fear. Fear of failure, greed to rise; a bad mixture, indicating an unstable temperament.

Nonetheless, since the Terrans had achieved only the sixth level in evolution and possessed both pedal and manual extremities and not vestigial but functional— they could be viewed only as animals. Hence Marshal Koli felt no qualms in the dreamy anticipation of the capture of Percy X; the Neeg-part commander would be mercifully killed and his virgin pelt would be removed, processed (including the head); glass eyes would be installed, though of course the organic teeth— if good—would be retained. What a magnificent wall-hanging! Or, if not that, if the pelt turned out to be furry enough, what a delicious rug to slither over!

In his villa on Ganymede, Marshal Koli possessed several excellent pelts already installed attractively, impressing the casual or formal visitor; he had expertly taken advantage of his location here on Terra throughout the war. Trophies constituted primary symbols of victory; they were not mere toys or art objects. They represented what had been achieved, and the wall-mounted pelt of Percy X would be the crowning acquisition.

. . . If he could acquire it before the termination of his position of authority.

From the Percy X file he lifted, with his jaws, a 3-D colour still photo of the Neeg and examined it with relish. What a fine forehead. And chin. The entire face squared off, full of strength, even beauty; no wonder the creature had risen to become the charismatic leader of all the remaining Neeg-parts in the mountains.

As soon as Miss Hiashi had contacted Percy X she

was to communicate, via a miniaturised transmitter concealed in the right cup of her bra, with Marshal Koli's office. And, continually, she would report concerning the whereabouts and activities of Percy X until such time as Koli saw fit to snap shut his trap on the Neegpart leader. Everyone would be happy. Miss Hiashi would have her recordings of the music of a vanishing cult and Koli would have his pelt. He felt admiration for the girl. It was just such boldness combined with guile that had gained her the high position she held in the show business world, together with the approval of the Ganymedian Bureau of Cultural Control.

Flicking on an intercom outlet before him he said, 'Any news from home? Has the Grand Council adjourned yet, or is it still in session?' Sometimes the confabulations of the Common Mind occupied weeks of squirming altercation.

His communications creech answered, 'No report yet, Marshal. I will inform you as soon as word comes through from our reps in the Council.'

It would take one Terran week for the ship from Ganymede, bearing the new civil administrator, to reach Tennessee following his appointment. And, added to this figure, one had to consider the administrator's procrastination, the bale of Tennessee being the unappetising prospect that it was. The appointee might in fact appeal, and litigation within the Common generally droned on for months.

Everything, to use the Terran expression, was A.O.K.

At that moment Marshal Koli's second-in-command, Colonel Mawoi, entered the room carried by his creeches. Communicating telepathically Mawoi said, 'Sir, may I make a minor point before you begin on other considerations with respect to the Percy X file?'

'Speak up,' Marshal Koli said irritably, aloud.

'I have recently, as you know, assisted in the processing of the file. There is one entry which perhaps you failed, due to the pressure of ...'

'What's the entry?'

Making no attempt to conceal his concern Colonel Mawoi said, 'The Neeg, sir; he is a telepath. A graduate of the school of the Bureau of Psychedelic Research. So of course he can't be spied upon, especially by someone such as Miss Hiashi, who would be physically close to him. He will instantly be aware of her mission and will, I imagine, not allow her to make a report on anything; he will very likely kill her on sight.'

With angry annoyance Marshal Koli said, 'Radio her instantly. Warn her; call her back. We can't throw away such a valuable contact for nothing.'

As the officer rushed away to carry out his order, Marshal Koli sighed gloomily.

'It would have been such a beautiful pelt,' he said at last, to himself and to the creeches within hearing.

Gus Swenesgard wiped his balding head dry with one energetic swipe of his red bandanna handkerchief and took a second look at the map in his hand. At the top of the map these words had been stamped: TOP SECRET! CLASS A MILITARY PERSONNEL ONLY! This, however, did not bother him. One of his Toms had found it in the ruins of the Oak Ridge Nuclear Power Station laboratories and now it was his to do with as he pleased.

'This is the place, all right,' he said, peering into the great hole which grew deeper by the minute. He had no automated digging equipment, but that didn't matter; he owned plenty of hard-working Toms and one good hollow-core shaft drill. And plenty of time.

'Aw come on, Gus,' his foreman Jack Haller yelled above the noise of the drill. 'We know you're not digging for any library. I mean, you got absolutely nobody fooled, so drop it.' He glared meaningfully at his employer.

'It says "library" on the map.' Gus waved the worn and crinkled document in Jack's general direction. It was true, though; Gus did not really believe that before the war the UN military had buried such a thing as a library here on his plantation. That was a code word for —something else.

It seemed so near that he could virtually taste it; his body ached for it.

'That map's Army, isn't it?' Haller demanded. 'And that's against occupation law, to dig up anything military. So you had to keep up this noise about libraries.'

Gus said, grinning, 'It's fifty thousand UN soldiers all armed with C-head rapid fire weapons. Waiting for the day to come when they reconquer the whole goddam planet.'

'And you're going to expose them?' Jack Haller stared at him. 'And bugger up the whole enterprise?' His stare became fixed with outrage. 'Where's your patriotism?'

'I was only joking.'

'What, then?'

'Girls. Fifty thousand virgins.' Gus winked.

Disgusted, his foreman stalked off to resume supervision of Toms and the digging rig.

To himself, so that Haller and no one else could hear, Gus murmured, 'I told you and you didn't believe me. So don't believe me; tough.' Because what he had said was true.

The UN had, in the final days of the war, selected

by computer a quantity of the finest womanhood—genetically speaking—from all the races of the planet, had introduced them to a homoeostatic subsurface totally sealed-off chamber . . . and then had gone to infinite trouble to destroy all records pertaining to the existence and location of the self-sustaining underground chamber—all this in case the invaders, now conquerors, had it in mind to abolish the human race in toto like the wriggly, slimy worms they were. However, the Ganymedians had no such plans; in point of fact, they had come in to occupy conquered Earth in the most deft, humane and circumspect manner—at least if their policies up to now constituted an index. So, Gus Swenesgard reasoned, this colony of first-class females served no purpose, and, since undoubtedly life was miserable underground, he would be doing them a favour by liberating them. They would be grateful. They would honour him. All in all it looked pretty good.

And he had plans. In exchange for releasing them—he did not know for certain how many women he would find, maybe a hundred, maybe two hundred—he wanted reciprocity. As his lawyer, Ike Blitzen, might put it.

Several of the really big plantation Burgers, like Chuck Pepitone and Jesus Flores, just to name the two closest, had whole colonies of wives, both coloured and white—although the coloured ones technically, by Tennessee law, comprised 'consorts', not wives. In fact this made up the essence of Burgerhood; in this lay the ultimate criterion. He knew that. Everybody knew that. Because women had become expensive. They sold, in the bales of the South, for much more than Toms; one could pick up a good brawny Tom for, say, fifty UN dollars, but a woman . . . well, that drew six times this price, assuming she came undamaged.

34

This, what he had here, this trove of girls—this constituted *currency*. Because the old pre-war UN money had become rapidly worthless as the Gany occupation authorities redeemed or withdrew it or whatever they did, and the junk they issued no sane mortal would touch, it was so obviously phony; as for instance whose pictures appeared on it? President Johnson? Stalin? No; the Gany had dipped into history and come up with full-face steel-engraved portraits of such freaks as Kant and Socrates and Hume and old-time non-heroes like that. For instance, the ten-dollar General Douglas MacArthur bill; in another month it would be gone entirely. And in its place somebody named Li Po, some sort of antique Chinese poet. It made a man blurk just to think about it.

So, anyhow, the occupation currency had become a racket by which the Ganys appropriated Terran valuables in exchange for worthless scrip. And everybody knew that, even up North where the worm-kissers, *wiks* for short, ran everything . . . that is, ran everything at the beck and call of the Gany military commanders, that being the nature of wiks.

Well, maybe his plantation was virtually the smallest in the whole bale of Tennessee; so what? It didn't matter, not after his drilling rig burst through into the mammoth sealed subsurface living-chamber designed to last a century and jam-packed with pristine womanhood in its choicest flower, safe from the Gany worms —or snakes, however you thought of them, whichever you liked least. Snakes were wriggly and had fangs and injected poison. And worms; well, worms were blind. If not worse. Having raised sheep he had seen parasitic worms . . . he had seen the bott fly. So to him the Ganys resembled worms, which was a lot worse than snakes.

'The hollow-core shaft,' Haller called to him suddenly. 'It's bringing up fragments of metal. It seems to be drilling into what looks like chrome steel.'

'How far down?' Gus asked.

'Exactly what you predicted: seven thousand feet.'

'Okay,' he said nodding. 'Use the fat shaft, the one we can descend in. I want to go down there. Me first; I'll tell you when you can follow.'

Shortly, in a harness suit, greased with a smelly plastic slime so that he would not become stuck, he found himself being lowered, cautiously, a lantern dangling below him to reveal the way. Directly behind him, just to make sure, followed a Tom with a dart pistol. In his left hand Gus gripped a rapid-fire phosphorous-cartridge revolver; in his right a fistful of documents identifying him as the legal Burger of the Fifteenth Plantation of the bale of Tennessee . . . so they would not mistake him for an invading Gany wik. Plus newspaper accounts published since Capitulation Day which recounted the lenient policies of the Ganys especially as regards the continuation of the human race: accounts which gave the lie to wartime scare stories of sterilisation plans and so forth.

He felt confident, even cheerful, and as he descended he hummed a jazzy tune, then wondered how it had happened to come into his head. Of course; he must have got it somehow from that girl Joan Hiashi whom he had met earlier in the day at his Olympus Hotel. And he wondered, idly, if she had managed to reach the unpacified hills and if so had Percy X's trigger-nutty zealots massacred her. If so that would be too bad; he had had plans for her.

At seven thousand feet his dangling lantern flashed broadly, into a cavern whose size could not be distinguished. And, as he swung downward, eager to reach the horizontal plane, he saw . . .

Electronic equipment, of some strange design such as he had never come across before. There seemed to be tons of components, wires and printed circuitry and helium batteries and transistors and peculiar crystalline objects of unguessable use glinting in the lantern light.

As he came to rest numbly on the floor of the cavern, he thought, *Then that about the girls, that was just to lure us into digging. In case we had become barbaric and didn't care about science. They conned us, those UN psychologists. They . . .*

His neck stung. An anti-personnel homotropic dart. He prayed, as his consciousness abruptly ebbed away and he stumbled to his knees, that it was just a stunner, not a metabolic toxin arranged for cardiac arrest. He managed to turn his head far enough to make out the Tom who had descended behind him. Why didn't the Tom do something? Then he realised the truth. It was the Tom who had fired the dart. Gus thought, he must be working for Percy X!

In Gus's earphones Haller's voice dinned in an anxious squeak, 'Hey, Gus; how come your dead-man's throttle's registering? What's wrong?'

It's registering, Gus thought dimly, *because I'm dead.*

A moment later Haller came hurtling down the shaft, spinning and twisting like a rag doll, and screaming.

4

As the ionocraft reached the northern border of the plantation, its articulation circuit creaked on and it declared, 'This is as far as I am licensed to go. I'll either have to alter course or deposit you here, miss. Take your choice.'

'I'd like,' Joan Hiashi said, 'for you to carry me to those hills over there.' She pointed.

'Go ahead and like away,' the taxi said, and veered to follow the perimeter of the plantation. The hills receded.

'Okay,' Joan said wearily. 'Let me off here.'

The ionocraft settled into a deserted, unclaimed marshland, miles from the hills. Getting out, Joan watched gloomily as the cab unloaded her recording equipment. She had been prepared, to some extent, for this; she had on high boots.

'Lots of luck, miss,' the taxi said, and, slamming its door, rose into the sky. She watched it until it had disappeared from sight and then she sighed heavily, wondering what came next.

Possibly she could walk the rest of the way to Percy's hills, but she could not carry the recording gear; it would have to be left here. In which case, why go to the hills at all?

A voice said, 'Miss Hiashi?'

She glanced around, startled, then realised that it came from the right-hand cup of her bra. 'Yes,' she said. 'What is it?'

'A small error,' said the voice which she now recognised as belonging to Marshal Koli. 'I neglected, in your briefing, to inform you that your friend, Percy X, has, since last being in contact with you, taken special intensive training at the school of the Bureau of Psychedelic Research.'

'So what?' She did not like the Gany's tone; he was trying, obviously, to break some sort of bad news indirectly.

'He's a telepath, Miss Hiashi.'

Seating herself on her recording gear she let the full impact of this news sink in. Finally she said, 'What am I going to do? Just wait for him to kill me? He may be zeroing in on me telepathically right this minute.'

'Be calm, Miss Hiashi,' the far-from-calm worm said. 'If you will set your bra transmitter to continuous broadcast we will be able to triangulate a fix on you in a short time and come to pick you up.'

'Pick me up?' she demanded. 'Or pick up what's left of me?' Savagely she unzipped her nylon coveralls, tore off her bra, placed the right cup on a rock and raised a booted heel above it.

'Miss Hiashi,' squeaked the bra, 'I warn you; if . . .' The voice ceased as she brought down her heel, hard, and heard a satisfying crunch as the delicate microscopic device disintegrated. The bra lay there, dead. She felt then a sudden sense of freedom. All the years of being a faithful co-operative wik—cancelled out in a moment's impulsive gesture. Or perhaps she might in time find her way back into the good graces of the authorities. But— she couldn't afford to let such thoughts cross her mind right now; Percy might be scanning them.

The noise of the motors. She glanced up. And felt fear.

Another ionocraft, even more seedy and in disrepair than the first, came clatteringly in over the treetops; it settled to earth, somewhat bumpily, a few yards from

39

her. Its door slid rustily half-open, stuck, shuddered; then at last, with a final surge of effort, moved fully aside to reveal a shabby, little-used interior that dated from years before the war.

'Are you from Percy X?' she asked. Her heart laboured.

'I'm private,' the ancient cab informed her tinnily. 'Not part of a fleet, like you have up North. I do what I like. For twenty UN dollars I'll convey you to the Neeg-parts. I've been following you, miss; I knew that creep of a wik ship would dump you off.'

'Are you safe to ride in?' She felt dubious.

'Sure. I own a very good Tom mechanic; I bought him with fares I saved up.' The cab added quickly, 'It's legal for a class-one homoeostatic mechanism to own a Tom; since the war, anyhow. Only most machines are too stupid to make such a major investment. Get within, miss.'

She clambered in. The cab loaded her gear into its luggage compartment with many alarming creaks and clankings. Joan zipped up her coveralls and, as the cab ascended, adjusted her makeup in anticipation of her first meeting with the leader of the Earth's last remaining resistance forces.

'Listen, don't be apprehensive,' the cab said. 'I ferry people to the hills all the time. I've got a monopoly; nobody else does it. That's how I earn a buck. I can't compete on the regular runs; I mean, I sort of smell bad, if you know what I mean. Some guy, when I was ferrying him, he said I smell like cat wee. Do you think so, or was he just trying to make me feel inferior?'

'He was trying,' Joan lied, 'to undermine your self-respect. For neurotic reasons of his own.'

'I generally carry Neegs who want to join Percy X;

they come from all over North America. From all over the world, in fact. But you're white; I mean, anyhow, you aren't coloured in the true sense of the word. Watch out for Percy's bodyguards, especially the man they call Lincoln, that he doesn't shoot you before you get a chance to open your mouth. I see you have recording gear, there.'

'I'm trying to record some of the Neeg-parts' music.'

'You're in the music business? Sing a jazz tune for me. To pass the time.'

Joan said. 'I don't sing.'

'You know *How High the Moon*?'

She grunted in affirmation.

'That's my favourite melody,' the cab continued. 'Remember how June Christy, back in 1950, used to sing it?' It hummed the tune as it flew toward the burgeoning hills. At last the hills lay directly below. The cab, breaking off its humming, said, 'Let's have the twenty UN dollars now. Before they kill you.' Its voice had suddenly become hard.

As she placed the bills in the proper slot the cab descended in nausea-producing close spirals.

'My whole descent circuit is gummed up,' it explained as it thumped onto the rough ground, bounced, at last came to a shuddering halt. 'Sorry. I'll give you back a dollar if you feel . . .'

'Keep it,' Joan said. And, opening the door manually, stepped out.

Wearing brown khaki uniforms, boots, with automatic side-arms, two Neeg-parts confronted her, both young and tough-looking. The cab hurriedly lurched into the air after first unloading, with frantic haste, her recording gear; it headed back in the direction from which it had come.

'Look at this,' one of the Neegs said conversationally to the other. 'A lily-skinner. What do you know about that.'

'Isn't she cute,' said the second, leering.

'You like to make the scene, baby?' the first asked.

His companion gave him a contemptuous shove. 'You'll get some white-man's disease from her, man. That's for sure.'

Joan said, 'Can you take me to Percy X?'

They continued to talk to each other as if she had not spoken. 'Well, what good is this white wik gal anyway?'

'She brought us some presents. Look at all that expensive electronic stuff.' Both men bent to examine it. 'Ought to be able to do something with that.'

'But the girl, we can't do nothin' with her.' The man spoke to Joan directly. 'I'm sorry, baby, but you can't have no last meal or blindfold or nothin'. We too busy for any of that crung.'

Speechless, terrified, Joan watched the man raise his laser rifle to his shoulder and aim it point-blank at her forehead while his companion chanted mockingly, 'This is it, baby; this is *it*.'

When Gus Swenesgard regained consciousness, the first sight that materialised before his clouded eyes was the snout, lizard eyes and worm-face of a Gany. Marshal Koli; he recognised him. *It's got to be a nightmare,* Gus thought groggily, rubbing his forehead and squinting.

But it wasn't.

Looking around, Gus discovered that he lay near the hole which he and his turncoat crew of rascally Toms had dug. Night had come; a sliver of moon cast just enough light to make the swarm of attendant creatures around Koli look even more like a bad dream. *How'd they get me back up to the surface?* he wondered. *I guess they can do anything,* he decided bleakly. *That's why they won; that's why they're here.*

'I'm not sorry for you, Mister Swenesgard,' Koli said in a hissing, cold voice. 'Do you know something, sir? You're finished. It would have been better for you if you had died in that cave as your foreman did. It is perfectly obvious what you anticipated doing. You have been, in direct opposition to the legal decrees of the Occupation Authority, searching for buried weapon-caches left by the defeated forces of your UN troops.'

'No,' Gus said thickly. 'It wasn't weapons; I wasn't looking for weapons.' He managed to sit up.

'Then what was it?' The voice bored at him, full of harshness.

Briefly, he thought of telling the worm. But he would never be believed. 'Never mind,' he said miserably. 'But on my mother's honour I wouldn't use weapons against you people.'

'Whatever you may have intended,' Marshal Koli snapped, *'the weapons are now in the hands of the Neegparts.* If they have been troublesome before, now they will be unbearable. You and that Joan Hiashi—you're both rebels. Therefore we will kill you both. And of course right away.' With his tongue Marshal Kli gave a signal; a huge, seemingly mindless creech grasped Gus in an unbreakable grip and began shoving him roughly toward the Gany's parked ship.

A moment later, inside the ship, Gus found himself pushed unceremoniously into an overstuffed Terran chair which the Gany had from somewhere appropriated.

He found himself sweating. But he had not given up; he dragged out his vast cotton bandanna handker-

43

chief and shakily mopped his balding head. 'You don't understand, Koli. I wasn't going to tell you, but I have —or I guess had—a military campaign in mind against the Neeg-parts. I was diggin' out those trick gadgets to use against Percy X. It's the truth, on my mother's honour. In fact, I was going to personally nail Percy for you, once and for all. You all don't know who your friends are.'

'I thought,' Koli said bitingly, 'that Miss Hiashi was our friend. But she destroyed contact-relations with us and has, no doubt, gone over to the Neegs by now. Taking with her valuable information about our operations in this area.'

'That Jap girl, that Hiashi; she was working for you?' He stalled for a time, trying to say something; his mind worked furiously. Out of the corner of his eye he could see three of the creeches putting in order some variety of machine. He had a suspicion, intense and immediate, that he knew what it did; he had seen pictures of such devices. The worms used it for skinning a man alive, slowly so as to preserve the skin. Once more he wiped the sweat from his face and thought, *Soon my hands will be secured and I won't even be able to wipe. And after a while I'll be another skin—pelt they call it—in Koli's famous collection.* 'You don't want me,' he said aloud as the creeches wheeled the machine over to him. 'I'm just small potatoes. You all want Percy, right? He's the Neeg; he's really giving you all trouble.'

'If I can't have him,' Koli said coldly, 'I'll just have to make do with you.' He gestured with his tongue for the creeches to hold Gus down.

'Wait,' Gus said hoarsely. 'You don't have to settle for me. You can have Percy X himself.' He hesitated. 'I can lead you right to him.'

44

The Gany general signalled his creeches to let Gus go. At least for the moment. 'How do you expect to do that?'

'When that Jap gal was in the hotel I took the liberty of patting her sweet little head.'

'I'm not interested in your sexual depravity, Mister Swenesgard.'

'But listen,' Gus said. 'I planted a little bitty micro-miniaturised transmitter in her hair; that's what I did.'

After an interval Marshal Koli began once again to visualise the beautiful pelt of Percy X; he perceived its appearance on the wall of his Ganymedian villa. 'Let the fool go,' Koli said to his creeches.

On his unmade bed, in his hotel room in Gus Swenesgard's none too luxurious tourist palace, Dr Paul Rivers sat and sweated. In theory, when the sun went down it was supposed to get colder, particularly in autumn. In fact, however, it had got even hotter.

Getting up, he moved to the window to stare moodily in the direction of the distant mountains. Somewhere out there could be found Percy X, the last symbol of man's greatness. And with him—the wik spy, Joan Hiashi. *If only I could warn him,* he reflected. *If only there existed some way by which I could reach him.* Reaching, he opened the window, as if this might help. But all it did was make more audible the tireless crickets and bring to his nostrils the smell of damp stagnation that hung over the little Southern town. It was, he realised, just as hot and muggy outside as inside.

Somewhere a far-off radio or TV set played tinnily.

The sound nudged an obscure piece of memory in his mind. Wasn't Percy X a telepath? Yes; according to the records Paul had been shown during his briefing Percy

X had graduated with honours from one of the Psyche-delic research schools. This meant that he could be reached, no matter where he was . . . but only, unfortunately, by another telepath. And Paul Rivers did not possess that talent.

On the other hand . . .

Quickly he put through a vidphone call to the central offices of his employer, the World Psychiatric Association. Shortly he found himself connected with Dr Ed Newkom, one of the planet's top authorities on communication.

'This is top priority, Ed,' he informed Newkom. 'I want the loan of a thought amplifier for a week or two.' Sometimes with luck, the device invented by Newkom could effectively double as an artificial telepathic booster —for a limited range, anyhow. 'I can't come and get it; you'll have to fly it down here.' He told Newkom, tersely, where he was.

'I don't trust any of the commercial transport systems.' Ed Newkom said. He hesitated. 'I'll—bring the thing down to you personally. With any kind of luck I'll be with you by morning.'

'Thanks, Ed.' He felt relief. 'The Association will pick up the tab on this.'

'This one is on me,' Ed Newkom said. 'Ever since reading your paper on propagation of group psuchosis I've wanted to see how you operate. I'm charging this trip up to education.'

After ringing off, Paul Rivers reseated himself on the bed, this time with a feeling of satisfaction. *I can't leave here*, he said to himself grimly, *but with any kind of luck my thoughts can!*

Mekkis gazed out of the window of the main passenger

lounge of the ship at the planet Earth, which now grew
larger by the minute. *There it is,* he breathed. *My bale.*
Tennessee.

Actually he could not clearly see it since the globe
had become partially hidden behind cloud formations.
But imagination filled in what the eye could not see.

He ordered another drink and, before lapping it, said
to his creeches, 'A toast, as they say on Earth. A toast to
the new emperor of Tennessee, Percy X.'

'A toast,' echoed the creeches. But only Mekkis
drank.

5

Joan Hiashi sat with her back against the wall of the
cave, studying the features of the huge black man who
crouched near her frying fish in a skillet over a small
electric heating unit.

'Percy?' she said softly.

'Yes.' The Neeg-part leader did not look at her, he
concentrated on what he held in his hand.

'Why did you stop that man from shooting me?'

'A thousand reasons and none,' Percy said gruffly.
'You and I studied Buddhism together; Buddha taught
us not to harm any living being. Christ said the same
thing. All those pacifist bastards agreed on it, so who am
I to argue with them?'

The bitter irony in his voice—she did not remember
it from the days when they had both been studying to be

47

ministers, each in his own faith. He had changed. Of
course. And she had, too.

'I know it isn't that simple now,' Percy added, turning
the fish over. 'We live in a universe of murderers. You
can't keep out of it, stay neutral, wait for the next world;
they won't let you, baby.'

'I know what you must have gone through,' she
began. But Percy broke in harshly.

'You do? You don't know a damn thing about me.
But I know all about you; I know all the worms you've
kissed. I know all the lies you've told—I knew when you
first started out to come here, to trap me for the Gany
military governor. Your mind is like a clear mountain
stream to me. That's my curse, baby; I can see it all.
Nobody can lie to me.'

'If you know,' she said carefully, 'then you know why
I did what I did. You know I had to do it. So you can
forgive me.'

'Sure, I forgive you. For everything. Not quite; except
for one thing. That I can't forgive.'

'What's that?'

'For you being alive, baby,' he said, still not looking
at her.

After they had eaten they made love, there in the soft
sand on the floor of the cave. Joan thought, as she lay
breathing deeply, afterwards, that it had been good to
make love to a man who hadn't crawled to anyone. She
had forgotten what it felt like. 'Is this what I really
came here for, subconsciously?' she asked him as she
toyed with his stiff, wire-like hair.

'I don't know. I can read you but I can't make excuses
for you.'

She pulled away from him with a jerk, feeling hurt
and puzzled.

48

'What's the matter, wik girl?' he growled. 'Don't you know you're supposed to love your enemies?'

'Stop throwing religion at my head.' She thought, now, how fine Percy would look on TV, what a great show she could build around him—if she could get back into favour with the Gany Bureau of Control. Then, abruptly, she realised that Percy was looking into her mind and seeing these thoughts, and she felt a moment of panic. How do you not think something? Just the effort of trying not to think it brings it more strongly into your mind!

'Once a wik, always a wik; right?' he said to her, fixing her with an unblinking stare.

'No, that's not true.'

'Don't lie to me.' He leaped to his feet, stood huge and black and dangerous as a bull in the ring, then began pacing restlessly back and forth, speaking in an intense monotone, now and then stopping to wave his arms, point a quivering finger, grimace savagely or shake his fist. 'What's the word "Neeg" mean, wik girl? Is it a race or is it a religion?'

'A race.'

'It's a religion, like being a Jew. Being white; that's also a religion. I can tell you in just one word what the white religion is.'

'What?' Joan said guardedly.

'Hypocrisy.' There was a long silence while Percy waited for this to sink in. Or perhaps he waited for a reply. But she said nothing. 'What's the matter, wik girl?' he demanded. 'Don't you know how to talk? Are you just going to sit there and take it when I call you a hypocrite?' Bending, he picked up his rocket dart pistol from the floor of the cave and levelled it at Joan's head.

'You'd kill me, just like that?'

'I saved your life; now it's mine, to do with as I please.'

'I didn't come here to do you any harm. I just wanted to collect folksongs for . . .'

'I don't know any songs,' Percy said curtly.

'Maybe it would help your movement if I broadcast some of your music on my show.'

'I told you I don't know any songs!' He waved his rocket dart pistol in emphasis. 'I've seen your show, and you know what I think of it?' He spat in the dust. 'It's *white* jazz you play and that's the same thing as nothing—meaningless noise, a big fake. You don't believe in what you play, do you? You have nothing but contempt for the people who like it and contempt for yourself for playing it.'

'It's a living,' she said tightly.

'I don't know why I don't shoot you; I'd be doing you a favour. God, I'd rather be dead than a gutless white jellyfish like you.' But he did not shoot, and she knew why. He had begun to enjoy tormenting her, searching with his telepathic ability through all the hidden parts of her mind, the places she herself never ventured into. 'I think its gratitude, that's what it is; I'm pathetically grateful to you for all you've done for my people, down through the ages—you've kept my people out of your world, kept them from becoming like you. Thank you, wik white girl; thank you. Thank . . .'

'Will you cut it out?' she snapped, angry at last.

'Backtalk? So there is some spirit in you. Maybe you've got a little Neeg blood in you, white wik girl. I'm going to do you a favour. I'm going to let you join me. I'm going to give you a chance to quit lying, get up off your belly and be an authentic human being. What do you say?'

'I don't know,' she said.

'That's just it; you don't know. But I'm willing to teach you; I'm willing to spend my priceless time and patience working with you on the remote chance there might be some trace of real colour hidden away in all that white mush you call your "personality". Listen; I know how you got brought up—don't you think I know what your people have done to you? I know how they had you fixed, like their dogs and cats; I know how they taught you to say 'thank you' when someone with money, occupation scrip or UN bills, steps on your face. I know how rotten you feel inside, empty and impotent and helpless. No wonder you need to pile up so much money to make people pretend to like you; no wonder you need all that fame to prove to yourself that you exist. Listen; I'm going to put a gun into your hands and give you a chance to kill a few of those white crunks that did this to you.' Abruptly he thrust his gun butt first into her hand, stood back and grinned.

'Suppose,' Joan said presently, 'I shoot you instead.'

'No. You don't have the guts.' But evidently he caught something deep in her mind, something marginal which even she could not perceive; as abruptly as he had given her the gun he yanked it back to his own possession. 'Lincoln,' he called, and his second-in-command appeared; he had, Joan realised, been listening and watching all this time. 'Take this white worm-kisser out of my sight. If I see it again I'll probably crush it under my heel.'

As Lincoln led her away she asked him, shaken and disturbed, 'What's wrong with him? Why does he rave on like that?'

Lincoln laughed sharply. 'Where's your woman's intuition, baby? Percy's been carrying your picture in his wallet for years—as long as I've known him. You're none other than his dear, darling, long-lost sweetie pie . . . and you're a worm-kisser. A *hopeless* worm-kisser. If you don't think that's funny you just don't have any sense of humour at all.'

Marshal Koli, Military Administrator of the occupied bale of Tennessee, said aloud to his staff, 'As you know, we have for months been contriving a stratagem with the purpose of snaring the Neeg-part leader, Percy X. In this connection we have, shall I say, agents within the 'part groups under fealty to Percy X. Thereby we have managed to ascertain to some degree his whereabouts at certain times.' He flicked his tongue at an impressive wall map which showed the bale, and, most specifically, the unpacified hill-areas controlled by both the Indian tribal remnants and the Neeg-parts.

On the map a luminous button, moveable, lay placed. The button represented the approximate current location of Percy X.

'Our operation,' Marshal Koli continued, 'is, as you know, called Operation Cat Droppings—a Terran idiom connected with some unpleasant task. And this has been unpleasant because it has taken too long.' At this point he drew himself almost entirely erect, balancing himself on his tail-tip in his determination to impart the seriousness of what he now proposed to declaim down the chain of command.

'Operation Cat Droppings,' he declared, 'will reach its crucial terminal phase at eleven p.m., bale of Tennessee time. Our crack commando teams, descending by means of individual air-pulsation tubs, entirely silently, will ring the spot where the malefactor is entrenched.' He paused and then said, 'This is the moment for which I have prepared during my entire period as Military Administrator of this bale. Each one of our predetermined, arranged-for tactical operations will, at eleven p.m., become operative. After that . . .' He flicked his tongue rapidly in agitation. 'Either we will have Percy X or we won't. In any case there will be no further chance.' Hastily he added, 'In terms of the *military* jurisdiction of this bale, I mean. What the civil administrator who follows me does I have no knowledge of.' *But,* he thought, *through our wiks who have infiltrated the Neeg-parts I do know Percy; a great deal about him, even though, thanks to Percy's telepathic ability, none of our wiks have been able to get close enough to kill him or even effectively spy on the operations of his inner circle of command.*

Touching a selenoid switch with his tongue he activated a servo-assist projector mounted on his desk; on the far wall, in 3-D and colour, appeared the image of Percy X, taken with a telescopic camera. Percy squatted in a leisurely, secure—or believed secure—parley with his sub-leaders.

'All Terrans tend, of course, to look alike,' the Marshal said. 'But observe the strong chin, the great wide smile of strength of this man. He is a superior Terran.' *The last,* he reflected, *to capitulate. And one, in scrutinising him, can readily see why.* 'To insure the success of Operation Cat Droppings,' he continued, 'I am offering, for this first and only time, this ultimate and critical fruition of all our painstaking planning, an incentive.'

All eyes in the room fixed rigidly on him.

'With incalculable generosity I am offering ten thousand tulebs for the creech who accomplishes the commando mission—income tax free, too.' He observed the gratifying servility revealed on each face; hunger for the reward, pitiless determination to be the one who earned it . . . and, seeing this, knew he had managed at this last critical hour, after so many false starts, to move in the right direction. This he had imbibed from Terran psychology books: how to motivate a person. 'Inform your subordinates,' he stated, 'that if this long-prepared-for coup fails, they will all be smunged. Do you comprehend, all of you who repose in soft felt-lined niches, what it means to be smunged?' He wove toward them menacingly, studying them with dour fierceness.

As one worm they nodded. Every member of the Ganymedian military had heard of the trial-less quasi-juridical procedures generally resulting in a fine of first magnitude and two centuries of smungedom on some airless rock in the asteroid belt.

And then there was the money. *Build an atomic pile to near-critical mass under their ani,* Koli said to himself, *and meanwhile dangle an addictive narcotic or the lettuce (a Terran term) before their noses: they'll come through. And . . .*

I've got to, too, he realised. *Now that I comprehend that the so-called 'wik' agent, that Joan Hiashi, was engaging in tarrydiddle from the start.* What if it got out that, in spite of his own telepathic ability, a mere Terran had outfoxed (also a Terran term) him? He still did not quite understand how she had done it. Plainly it was one thing to read a mind and another to understand it, particularly if it was the mind of some member of an alien race.

But now, thanks to the animal craft of that fawning toady, Gus Swenesgard, she'll lead me to him in spite of herself. If not, I'll be the one who got used . . . by her.

'The operation,' he declared, 'will develop in the

54

usual pattern which has been, up to now, so successful in other areas of this planet. First, unmanned homotropic missiles of the dart variety will be released from a satellite passing overhead; they will not kill, only stun. Then, when the 'parts are rendered harmless . . .' He droned on and on. 'And in conclusion,' he wound up, 'let me warn you: Percy X's pelt must be absolutely intact. No burns, holes, tears, rips, thin spots; there must be no defacement of any kind. You understand? The highest sort of aesthetic values are involved in this matter; this is not a mere political or military operation —this is, first and foremost, a great art-treasure hunt.'

It had become cold. Cold and damp and foggy; the Tennessee hillside forest poked up indistinctly. The Neegparts, however, could not risk building a fire; the Ganys had sensitive heat detectors that would zero in on a camp-fire in an instant, even through the overcast. Instead they huddled together for warmth, arms and legs intertwined, blankets and threadbare sleeping bags spread over them to retain as much as possible of the precious body-heat.

And they talked together quietly, or slept—although most had picked up the necessary habit of sleeping in the daytime and waking to alertness at night.

Joan Hiashi and Percy X lay in the midst of the mound of human flesh, sharing an oversize overcoat.

Holding the girl loosely in his arms, Percy said, 'It takes danger, the deadly kind, to make men touch each other. But when they do, it's good; it's the finest thing there is. But we humans have always been afraid of each other. We've wanted to think ourselves as spirits without bodies, or minds that triumphed over matter, not as a herd of animals huddling together for warmth. I'm thankful to the Gany's for . . .'

'Christ, it's cold,' Joan said, through chattering teeth.

'Be glad you can feel the cold. At least you can feel *something*.'

Someone in the heap began humming.

'Won't the Gany sound detectors pick that up?' Joan asked.

'There's a wind,' Percy said. 'The wind and the sounds of the birds and animals make it hard for them to track on sounds.'

Another voice joined in, and another and another. She had never heard anything like it before. Long sobbing moans that slid up and down the scale without a break, superimposed over a rhythm more implied than stated, a rhythm that seemed to suggest the beating of a vast communal heart. There seemed to be no preconceived melody, and each voice joined in and ceased wherever the singer chose.

Now more voices joined in. The tempo increased. Some of the men began to slap out a rhythm with the palms of their hands against their bodies. Joan felt the music's beauty as a pain in her chest. Her mind resisted, thrashing like a man drowning, but her emotions became caught up in the music and flung wildly downwards, like a stick in the rapids.

'Go ahead,' Percy said gently. 'Record it.' Evidently he knew that she wore a microminiaturised tape recorder disguised as a wristwatch. 'Take it with you when you go back. It doesn't matter after all.' He, too, seemed moved by the music. 'If those worms finally manage to finish us off, at least our song will still be around to make you wiks uncomfortable, to remind you what a man sounds like.' With tenderness he ran his

56

hands through her hair . . . and froze. He had come across something small, round and metallic, something in her hair.

'Ouch,' she cried as he jerked it loose.

Quickly, expertly, he examined it by matchlight. 'A radio,' he muttered, then threw it as far as he could into the darkness. Jumping to his feet he shouted to his men, 'Move out! Move out! Scatter! This damn wik girl was bugged! They may be closing in on us right this minute!'

Without a moment's hesitation they scattered, guns at the ready. Joan ran also, after Percy's retreating back. 'Don't leave me here,' she gasped, stumbling, almost falling in the mist-shrouded darkness.

A light appeared in the sky, small, like a falling star, yet it had to be closer than a falling star.

'Look out, Percy!' Joan shouted. It was a miniature tapered autonomic dart, descending at spectacular velocity, and seeking just one person, Percy X.

Lincoln raised his laser rifle and, with a skill that showed an almost automatic reflex, he shot the descending dart out of existence.

'Another,' Percy snapped. 'To the right.' He did not sound frightened, but his voice had become speeded up and shrill. 'A third. Too close, too close; we can't get them all.' He said it factually, without the warmth even of despair: no time now for that meagre emotion, no time even to give up. Percy X fired, almost as Lincoln did; the two Neegs fired again and again and still the rain of black, homotropic dots descended. A Gany weapon, Joan realised. From the war. The *Shaft*, it had been called. It had, alone, taken out on an individual basis, one by one, a vast number of highly-placed, essential Terran technicians and military leaders.

Kneeling, Percy swiftly unstrapped a small packet from his calf. With a violent scratching motion against the rough soil he ignited it; the mechanism flashed and a cloud of noxious denseness flowered until the sky disappeared.

The Shafts themselves would be unaffected. But their tropisms would be abolished; they would have no destination and would begin to strike at random. Unless one or more had already come too close, had passed the stage in which the tropism defined the direction of flight.

Too late for Lincoln; in the gloom Joan heard him cry out and fall. Then Percy too shouted one brief strangled cry before toppling to the weed-infested ground. No dart had been set for Joan's particular cephalic index, so the weapons left her alone—assuming that none of the wild ones got her at random. Operating by the sense of touch alone she moved quickly to where she had heard Percy fall. *It's my fault*, she said to herself bleakly.

No time existed, however, to brood about that. Somehow, with a strength she never knew she had, she managed to half-drag, half-carry him a few yards; panting painfully, her knees wobbling, she stumbled through the invisible weeds, slid on shards of rock and dirt particles, down a slope, away, with no direction in mind, only the knowledge that she had to act rapidly. Blindly, without any real hope, she slithered and slid and hurried as best she could, dragging the inert but not dead—she knew the Shafts; they did not generally carry freights of toxins—to some other, vague, unknown place.

Ahead, a shape, upright, moved. *A Neeg-part,* she thought with relief. She said gaspingly. 'They got Percy with a Shaft; I'm trying to get him out before the next step.' She panted for breath.

The upright, metal-encased figure, like some artificial chitinous reflex entity, said, 'I am the next step.' It lifted a hand weapon and aimed it at Joan. 'This does not stun,' it said in faultless but overly-precise English. 'You are my prisoner, Terran. As is he.' It gestured with a manual extremity toward the inert figure lying before Joan. 'Most especially he.' The slotted eyes glowed and projected a beam of illumination, assisting it in making its visual scan which would be transmitted to Gany military operation GHQ. The scan, already, was being relayed; she heard the hum.

Bending over Percy she snatched the hand gun from his belt; within the mass of metal confronting her dwelt a creech and she meant to kill the thing or be killed by it. At pointblank range she fired.

The bullet, ringingly, bounced off the creech's polished armour. Harmlessly. The thing did not even appear to notice; it continued with its scan of Percy's features.

Joan Hiashi emptied the gun futilely at the towering hulk before her, then threw the weapon at it. And then stood helpless, waiting, the still-inert Percy X in a tumbled, dead-doll heap before her.

6

Marshal Koli's private secretary crept towards him, stood on tip-tail and delivered a confidential message. 'Sir, there is a person named Mekkis, a Ganymedian, who claims to be the civilian administrator who is to relieve you.'

Time, evidently, had run out—and sooner than he had expected. But perhaps with a little adroit stalling he could gain a few extra hours . . . enough to complete Operation Cat Droppings. Koli slid his way across the office, opened the door to the waiting room—using the low-placed tongue switch that responded to no tongue but his—and surveyed his replacement.

Outside reposed a grey, sombre-looking compatriot, a man of obvious and durable ability; much older, in fact, than the Marshal himself. He reposed well: with dignity, and did not bother to notice the existence of the spools of FUN-E tapes available for the visitor; nor did he gaze at the several attractive, well-groomed secretaries at work. Beside him lay a thick briefcase with leather neck strap for carrying. And outdoors in the well-lit courtyard waited a team of flyers, their wings rising and falling rhythmically in a semi-doze.

Well-trained, Koli reflected. *Their master is a good one; they don't flap about causing a disturbance. Clearly a high genetic breed. Undoubtedly costing their owner a fortune.* Therefore this indubitably was Koli's civilian replacement. 'Mr Mekkis?' Marshal Koli inquired.

The head whipped; the tongue protruded, licking the air with intensity as the wide-set eyes flamed, a dismal and perplexing glance, as if Mekkis did not quite see him, saw instead beyond—and not yet spatially. It was, he realised, as if this man possessed the capacity to imagine one's entire life-track, one's full destiny; perhaps, he decided, age had something to do with it. *Wisdom,* he thought. *There is wisdom, not sheer knowledge as on the memory spools of a computer, lying behind these green, faceted eyes.* He felt uncomfortable.

60

'Do you intend to take possession of the desk immediately?' Koli inquired. He thought once more of Percy X's rich, thick, virgin-fur pelt; it had now faded to the dimensions of a dream.

'Frankly,' Mekkis said, 'I'd like to get the transfer of authority over right now, so I can get some rest. I didn't sleep well on the ship.'

'Come into my office,' Koli said, leading the way. 'A dish of authentic Spanish sherry.' As one of his batmen poured the two saucers full he explained, 'From Puerto Santa Maria, Spain. A niña—light golden and medium dry.' He added, between laps, 'I consume it at room temperature, but it can also . . .'.

'Your hospitality,' Mekkis said after a few polite laps at the dish of sherry, 'is singular. Now, as to the transfer of authority.'

'There are the fighter planes.'

Mekkis, astonished, said, 'My briefing didn't mention any fighter planes.'

'Well, they're not real fighter planes; they're models, you see. World War One.'

'What is "World War One"?' Mekkis asked.

Slithering to a long low polished wood table, Marshal Koli said, 'These are of a rare twentieth-century plastic, injection productions which reproduced details so minutely as to be beyond compare.' As he bade an attendant to pick up a model he said, 'Unfortunately, the knowledge of how to manufacture this plastic has died out. Allow me to trace the development of fighter aircraft during the First World War.' He flicked his tongue at the first model, held up to Mekkis for inspection by the assistant. 'This was the first true fighter, the Fokker Eindekker. One wing, you see?' He showed the wing, with its supporting struts.

'Hmm,' Mekkis said, in a neutral tone; he had been trying for a telepathic scan of the Marshal but a scramble pattern blocked the view. Nothing could be made out except a vague jumble of airplane images. *Maybe*, Mekkis thought, *it's not a scramble pattern; maybe that's how he really thinks.*

'The Allies had nothing to match the Fokker Eindekker I, II or III until December of 1915.'

'How,' Mekkis asked, 'do they arrive at dates here?'

'It is based on the birth of Jesus Christ, the Sole Begotten Son of God.'

'The way you talk,' Mekkis said dryly, 'one would think you'd gone native. Do you believe in this God business?'

Marshal Koli drew himself up to half-height, wove back and forth with dignity and said, 'Sir, for the last two years living here on Terra I have been an Anglo-Catholic. I take communion once a month.'

Mekkis quickly turned the conversation back to the relatively safe topic of model airplanes. New converts to these native mystery cults could sometimes wax quite fanatical. 'What's this plane here?' he asked, closing his jaws over the tail-section of a biplane.

Marshal Koli shut his eyes and said, 'Would you allow my trained assistant to handle the items of this rare, even unique, collection, sir? By wousling them you cause me great mental anguish.'

'My pardons, of course.' Mekkis set the biplane down carefully, and there was not a toothmark on it.

The Marshal launched out on the subject of World War One aircraft once again, and half an hour passed before Mekkis managed to break into the flow long enough to reintroduce the topic of transfer of authority.

'Enough, Marshal; I would like to take command of this bale . . .'

'Wait.' Koli touched a wall-stud and a section of the wall rolled aside—revealing further rows of scale model planes. 'This section of my collection is devoted to the famous planes between the First and Second War. Let us initially consider the Ford Tri-motor.'

The attendant, as he showed the Ford Tri-motor to Mekkis, said reverently, 'He also has a complete collection of World War Two planes.'

'I . . . am overwhelmed,' Mekkis managed to say.

Matter-of-factly, Koli continued, 'I cannot of course transfer these incredibly valuable models to Ganymede; they would be smashed beyond repair—you know the slipshod way in which our homoeostatic unmanned cargo carriers land.' He eyed Mekkis. *I am therefore leaving my collection, all of it, even that of the World War One fighters, to you.'*

'But,' Mekkis protested, 'suppose I break one of the planes?'

'You will not,' the Marshal said quietly. And that, evidently, was that. There the subject ended.

Telepathically, Mekkis all at once detected some sort of confusion outside. 'The creeches have captured someone,' he said. 'Better have them bring him in.'

Koli grew pale. The beautiful pelt was now so near, yet still out of reach. 'Surely it would be better to wait until . . .'

'If this is how you habitually act I'll take authority as of now. Officially I have been in charge here since my arrival.' He sensed that Koli did not wish him to know of the disturbance outside. And for that reason he insisted on knowing.

'Very well,' Koli muttered.

Mekkis had lifted out a model of a 1911 pusher-type biplane when Marshal Koli returned from his errand, breathing erratically. With him appeared a Terran, a dark one, almost black. A Neeg.

'Administrator,' Koli said sharply, 'in an operation put into motion by myself before you arrived to relieve me of my desk as supreme authority in the bale of Tennessee I achieved this final, all-out coup, an ensnarement bordering on the divine. Do you know who this Terran is?'

Mekkis made an attempt to tear himself away from the scale models of antique aircraft. He found himself unable to. One—not strictly a model but a 2-D photograph, non-colour—showed a flimsy, ancient plane landing on the deck of a ship; he read the Terran words beneath it and learned that this, on January 18, 1911, constituted the first landing . . .

Going to the far side of the office in a furious slithering of almost hoop-like rolling, Marshal Koli touched stud after stud in the cabinets there, cabinets which Mekkis had not even noticed, let alone investigated. 'Ancient automobiles,' Koli said savagely. 'From the 1898 Peugeot on. Hours, days; and once you get finished with these there's my scale model steam locomotive collection in office 4-A.' He turned, slithered ragingly back; Mekkis had rarely seen a fellow worm so in the grip of his thalamus. 'I insist that you make official note of my capture of the leader of the Neeg-parts, Percy X, and that you certify that I am therefore the sole and unqualified owner of this quatropodia Terran entity, to do with as I want!'

Mekkis caught a thought that smacked of treason flashing through Koli's otherwise carefully scrambled mind; Koli had wondered whom, in the case of a showdown, the troops would obey, Mekkis or himself. He said aloud, 'You may take full credit, Marshal. It's clear to me that you are what is known as a collector . . . a definite sub-variety of individual typology. Even your adoption of this obscure Terran religion could be regarded as a manifestation of the collector instinct. Let me guess, sir. You want the pelt of Percy X. For a wall-hanging. He would indeed make an attractive decoration, teeth and all—right, Marshal? There is, on many highly masculine, fully-ripened, sexually-endowed Terran males, a vestigal covering of fur, especially on the chest region and—in other areas.'

Everyone in the room stared at him and then, in the silence, Percy X laughed. A hot, rich laugh, devoid of the slightest trace of sardonic or malicious overtones. And at the same time he grinned directly at Mekkis, and it was a personal, shockingly intimate grin; it was a creature-to-creature grin.

For the life of him Mekkis could not imagine what so delighted the captured partisan leader; he felt mystified and at the same time fascinated at an ethnic response both so unexpected and so arcane. He tried to read the human's mind and found a perfect scramble pattern waiting for him. That could only mean that Percy X was one of those very rare types, a Terran telepath.

'Can I have him?' Koli said tensely.

'No.'

'Why not?'

Mekkis said, 'I have other plans for this biped, Marshal. Plans that I'm sure you would oppose if you knew about them.' Addressing the guards he continued. 'Place this captured Terran in comfortable surroundings where proper interrogation can take place. Tomorrow, when I am rested, I have various matters to talk over with him.'

As Percy X was led out the creech who had made the capture said, 'Mr Administrator, we found another Terran with him at the time of capture. A female, of the white strain—that is of the strain ordinarily hostile to the Neeg-parts. Dermal dye-codes and other identification make it clear that she is the well-known television personality . . .'

'Later,' Mekkis said, and felt weary.

'Shoot her,' Marshal Koli rasped.

'No,' Mekkis countermanded. 'Place her in the custody of . . .' He could not remember the name of the counter-intelligence agency operating here on this colony world. 'Of the customary bureaux involved,' he finished lamely.

'She's a traitor,' Koli said. 'She must be shot.'

'Koli,' Mekkis said, 'contain yourself. There is an old saying here on Earth, I understand. "A worm which turns once can turn again", or something like that. The artful use of traitors is the secret of bloodless conquest, and I am not fond of violence.' He had begun thinking back to his briefing on Terran psychology. A place existed on this planet, if he recalled correctly, which the occupation forces fancifully called the 'School for Wiks', run by a Terran psychologist named Balkani. The girl could be sent there right away, and as for Percy—he would talk to him first, scan him, test him out.

Mekkis considered himself a gambler. But he liked to stack the deck.

Later, after he had rested, Administrator Mekkis had the Terran brought to his office; he confronted Percy X alone, without the annoying presence of Marshal Koli.

66

'What do you want out of me?' Percy demanded, not seating himself.

'Understanding,' Mekkis said. 'You are a telepath. If any human can bridge the gap between our two races a telepath should be able to do it.'

'I mean specifically,' Percy said tautly. 'What do you want me to do?'

The worm made what might have been a shrug, then said, 'Join us.'

Percy caught a glimpse, in the worm's mind, of himself, Percy X. Percy X, the hunted and hated Neegpart, as Emperor of the whole bale of Tennessee. There he sat, ruling over all the whites, even over some of the lower caste Ganymedians.

It would have been impossible to offer Percy anything that more exactly fitted his own ambitions.

'I see that you understand,' Mekkis said, with just the right shade of eagerness in his voice. 'What is your decision? Remember that you need not make up your mind in haste; you may take days to think it over. Weeks, in fact. I, personally, have plenty of time. But while you wait our forces will have no choice but to continue their police action against your people in the hills. Every day that you delay will mean the unavoidable loss of more lives plus the . . .'

Without warning Percy X leaped.

Mekkis jerked sideways, trying to escape, but it was no use; the great black Terran landed on him with his full weight, almost knocking him unconscious, then Mekkis felt powerful fingers close over his windpipe and squeeze, squeeze the life out of him. A moment before he blacked out the creeches descended in a howling, squealing horde on the Earthman's back and dragged him off.

'Kill him! Kill him!' the creeches screamed hysterically, but Mekkis gasped out, 'No, just hold him down. It's all right. He is just a little high-spirited, that's all.' Though he felt badly bruised by the struggle Mekkis managed to retain his composure and slipped back into his niche behind the desk.

'I regret having to do this,' Mekkis said to Percy, his voice shaking only slightly, 'but I'm afraid that before we can continue this discussion you will need a little psychotherapy to discourage these violent tendencies. However you will be happy to learn that you will be treated by a man often regarded by Terrans and Ganymedians alike as the greatest analyst of our time, Dr Rudolph Balkani.'

For just a fraction of a second Percy X dropped his scramble pattern; Mekkis was able to glimpse a swift flash of terror in the Neeg-part's mind.

What a pleasant surprise, Mekkis thought with satisfaction. *I had begun to believe this brute was afraid of nothing.*

In the hushed silence of Paul Rivers' seedy hotel room Dr Newkom slowly, carefully lifted the telepathic amplifier from Paul's head. 'Did you get through to Percy X?' Newkom asked.

'Yes.' Paul Rivers nodded. 'But only to listen; I made no attempt to contact him. That excitement a little while back—creeches brought him in to the Gany military.'

'Too bad,' Newkom said. 'We should have started getting to him sooner.'

'This gadget of yours is still too highly selective and directional,' Paul said. 'I don't know why I expected to achieve contact at the first crack.' *And now we've had it*, he thought. *If anyone can break a man, it's Balkani.*

68

Rudolph Balkani belongs to a school of therapy I wouldn't touch with a ten-mile pole, but I have to admit he gets results. It's always easier and more impressive to tear things down rather than to build them up or even to sustain them. A human being takes a long time to grow, to mature, but it only takes a moment to damage and destroy him.

And, he thought, *a wik Percy will be even worse than a skinned one. When the saviour sells out . . .*

'You can't win them all,' Newkom said. He shut off the power supply of the amplifier and prepared to leave.

'I'm not finished yet,' Paul said.

'But they've got Percy.'

Paul said, 'Want to go to Norway with me?' Without waiting for an answer he began quickly and efficiently packing his suitcase.

7

Coming out of the bright sunlight into the dark hallway Joan Hiashi could hardly see where she was going.

The guard said, 'This way, Miss Hiashi,' and opened a door for her. The room she entered through this door seemed even darker than the hallway had been, but she could make out the figure of a bearded, slightly over-weight and balding man who walked up to her and thrust out his hand.

'Balkani is my name, Miss Hiashi,' he said in a businesslike way. 'Dr Rudolph Balkani. The depth analyst.' They shook hands and Balkani offered her a chair. It turned out to be a psychiatrist's couch, but she did not lie down; she sat watching the dim shape of the psychiatrist with suspicion. 'What is your religion, Miss Hiashi?' he asked as he casually filled his pipe.

'Neeg-part,' she said defiantly. 'If I wasn't Neeg-part I wouldn't be here.'

'But on all the forms you have ever filled out before now you've listed your religion as Buddhism. Have you abandoned Buddhism?'

'There were no Ganys on Earth when Buddha lived,' Joan answered. 'Now a person is either a Neeg-part or nothing.'

'I tend to take a different view, Miss Hiashi.' He paused to light his pipe. 'I don't regard Neeg-partism as a religion at all, but rather as a mental disease, a subtle form of psychic masochism.'

'And you intend to cure me of it, is that right?'

'With your cooperation.'

'I'm sorry,' Joan said, 'but cooperation is one thing you're not going to get.'

Balkani raised his eyebrows. 'How hostile you are, Miss Hiashi. You have nothing to fear from me; after all, I'm a doctor,' He allowed a stream of fragrant smoke to drift from his mouth. 'Do you feel guilty, Miss Hiashi?'

'No,' she said. 'Not particularly. Do you?'

'Yes.' He nodded. 'For being alive. We should all be dead, every man, woman and child on this planet; we should have given our lives down to the last person rather than surrendering to the Ganys. Don't you think that's true, Miss Hiashi?'

She had not expected to hear something of this sort from a wik psychiatrist. For a moment it occurred to her that this man might be her friend, might really be someone she could trust.

70

'We've been bad, Miss Hiashi,' Balkani continued. 'And so of course we should be punished. We yearn for punishment; we need it; we can't in fact live without it. Right, Miss Hiashi? So we turn to a futile cause like Neeg-partism and that fills this deep and fundamental need in us all, the need for punishment. But there is, in us, an even deeper need. It's for oblivion, Miss Hiashi. Each of my patients, each in his own way—they all want to cease to be. They all want to lose themselves.

'And how is that possible, Miss Hiashi? It's impossible, except in death. It's an infinitely receding goal. And that is why it produces addiction. The seeker after oblivion is promised by drugs, by drink, by insanity, by rôle-playing, the fulfilment of his dream of nonbeing . . . but the promise is never kept. Only a little taste of oblivion is permitted; only enough to rouse the appetite for more. Participation in a lost cause, such as the Neeg-part movement, is only one more, slightly more subtle, form of this universal lemming-like drive for oblivion.'

At the end of his tirade Dr Balkani had become panting and sweating; his face shone with unnatural redness.

'If you really believed all that,' Joan said, 'you wouldn't have to shout so loud.' And yet he frightened her. And what he said next frightened her even more.

'Wouldn't you like to know the new therapy which I have planned out to cure these oblivion addicts?' Balkani demanded. 'The new technique which I've spent so many years perfecting—which I am at last ready to test?'

'No,' she said; the fanatical glow in the doctor's eyes filled her with alarm.

'I'm going to give them,' he said softly, 'just what they want, what they most desire. *I'm going to give them oblivion.*' He pressed a button on his desk; two wheeled attendant robots entered. Carrying a restraining suit. She screamed and fought. But the robots had too much strength, too much weight, to be retarded by even her most violent efforts.

Balkani watched, breathing heavily, his hands, as he grasped his now unlit pipe, shaking slightly.

Most of the locks in the Psychedelic Research prison were combination locks, though they had taken the trouble to install a key-operated lock on Percy X's room. By the end of the first week Percy had read the combinations to all the locks in his area from the minds of the guards and memorised them. The fact that all the guards thought in Norwegian had stopped him for a while, until he hit on the trick of simply watching what they did through their own eyes whenever they dialled a combination.

Escape posed difficulties even for a telepath. But not impossible ones, he reasoned. True, he would have to make a try at getting Joan Hiashi out, too . . . but there had to be a way; theoretically a way existed by which to accomplish everything.

He lay on his cot, half-dozing, when a voice spoke in his mind. 'Are you Percy X?' it asked.

'Yes.' He put himself on guard instantly, expecting a trap—even though his usually reliable intuition told him that this came from someone friendly to him. 'Who are you?' he thought back in response.

'Someone who wants to get you out of there. But in case we can't it's best that you don't know my name. They might find ways of making you reveal it.'

A guard passed by the cell; Percy focused on him to see if he had telepathic abilities. He had not.

'Do you know exactly where you are?' the voice in his mind continued. 'You are in Norway, on Ulvöya

72

Island, a few miles outside of Oslo. We are set up in Oslo, not far from you. While probing around Ulvöya Island, trying to locate you, I picked up rather ominous information. They plan to use Joan Hiashi against you.'

'How?' he thought back tensely.

'They're involved in performing a psychiatric experiment on her; at least that's what they call it.'

'Can . . .' Percy thought with effort. '. . . you do anything?'

Paul Rivers' answer was gentle but unavoidably cruel. 'We're not ready to make our move yet. At present there's not a thing we can do.'

Just then the doorbell jingled in Paul's little fortune-telling parlour; he snatched the telepathic amplifier from his head and said in a low voice to Ed Newkom, who sat nearby monitoring the controls, 'Ring up Central in New York on the scrambler vidphone and ask them to hurry up with that hardware I ordered when I left the States. If it doesn't come through soon they might as well forget it. It'll be too late.'

Ed slipped out into the back room and Paul, before opening the door, made sure that the hi-fi with its Hindu music was loud enough to drown out any stray noises his partner might make. He then passed on into the front parlour and prepared to greet a customer of their alleged enterprise—their cover while they worked here, trying to release the Neeg-part leader and Joan Hiashi.

Mekkis studied once more the faded and tattered military documents before him on the desk. Things did not look good.

'The weapons found by Gus Swenesgard,' he informed his precog creech, 'are described here in the most vague terms, but appear to have some sort of effect on the mind. That might account for the strange reports we've been getting from the units assigned to the mopping-up operation against the Neeg-parts who still, in spite of the loss of their leader, unreasonably continue to hang on.'

'Invisible men,' muttered the precog. 'Men turning into animals. Unnatural monsters that form and unform without warning and do not show up on radar. All part of the same thing—the coming darkness. Oh, sir; your time grows short. The Nowhere Girl will be born somewhere on this planet within the next few days. She is the first sign of the end.'

'Can you tell yet who she is?' Mekkis demanded, momentarily losing control of himself in his agitation. 'Or where she is?'

'That I cannot say, but once she dwelt here in this bale. I no longer sense her close by.'

'She must have escaped into the hills,' Mekkis muttered. He returned, then, to the study of the documents before him. How could Gus Swenesgard, he asked himself, have been so stupid as to allow such deadly devices to fall into the hands of the Neeg-parts? That took more than ordinary dullness, the kind of stupidity that can only result from long practice and hard study.

And yet this same man had played an important part in the capture of Percy X.

'I must meet this Gus Swenesgard,' Mekkis said aloud. He had hoped to have some report from the Psychedelic Research people on Percy X long before now. What were they doing there in Norway, anyhow? Unless the Terran they called Balkani could deliver him a functioning and docile Percy X and soon, the mop-up operation against the Neeg-parts might drag on for

74

years. Or might abruptly turn against the Gany occupation forces. Those weapons . . .

And this Balkani. It was he, it seemed, who had evolved the principles on which these mind-warping devices worked. And he who had worked out a technique for training the ordinary telepathic powers of certain gifted Terrans so that they almost equalled in power an experienced Ganymedian member of the Great Common.

And he to whom uncooperative Earthmen got routinely sent—to be turned into useful wiks.

'Balkani, too,' Mekkis mused aloud. 'I must meet him.'

On impulse he pressed the key of his intercom with his tongue, sent an order out for a full search of nearby reference libraries for the works of this famous psychiatric figure; they might, he reflected, make highly interesting reading.

'You wished to see Gus Swenesgard?' the Oracle demanded, interrupting his meditations. 'He is on his way; presently he will be here.'

Ten minutes later Gus indeed sat waiting in the outer office. He did not seem surprised when he received the command to enter; with a snappy salute he ambled in to face Mekkis, the picture of self-satisfied certitude.

'You can drop that saluting now, Mr Swenesgard,' Mekkis greeted him caustically. 'The military occupation of this bale has terminated.'

'Yes sir,' Gus said, with vigour. 'What I'm here for is . . .' He coughed nervously. 'I have some information, Mr Administrator, sir.'

A quick scan of the man's mind proved interesting; Mekkis found Gus to be shrewd and highly cunning—qualities nobody would ever have suspected on the basis of his outward, physical appearance. If Percy X did not come through, perhaps this individual might.

'I got spies, see, among the Neeg-parts,' Gus said, wiping his nose with the back of his arm. 'And they tell me a lotta funny things are going on up in the hills. Those gadgets they got out of the cave; well, they are really humdingers, let me tell you.'

'What is a "humdinger"?' Mekkis asked, worried.

'Well, you know, Mr Administrator, sir, they got some mighty funny effects on people's minds. Makes people see things that ain't there and not see things that are there, if you know what I mean, and they're getting kind of cocky with them. Like one of them black devils walked into my front room, invisible, and painted a black cross on my wall, right in front of my very eyes. I thought I'd been hitting the bottle a little too heavy, sir, but it was still there the next day. So I guess it must have been real.'

'What does that mean, a black cross?'

'Means they're going to kill me if I don't do what they say; that's what it means.' Gus looked unhappy.

'I'll provide you with protection,' Mekkis said shortly.

'I always heard that the best defence is a good offence. Why don't you provide me with a little tactical force?' The drawling, rustic accent had vanished, now; the man's tone bristled with direct intent. 'Some ionocraft bombers and autonomic darts and let me go up into those hills after those rascals.'

'I already have several units in the hills. What could you do that they aren't already doing?'

'I could win,' Gus said quietly. 'Where you fellers, no offence intended, are likely to just keep batting around up there 'till hell skids over with ice. I know the hills. I have spies. I understand how the Neeg mind works. I can locate where they got those weapons hidden, those mind-warping things.'

Routinely Mekkis glanced into the man's mind—and started in surprise at what he found there. Absolute deception: Gus intended to find the weapons, all right—but he would keep them for himself.

For a moment Mekkis pondered. Gus could of course be bugged and even provided with some variety of remote control instant-kill device. Even though his motives were impure perhaps he could locate the weapons and defeat the Neegs, where the Gany occupation forces had failed. Then, at the instant in which Gus believed he had everybody fooled, the remote control kill-unit, hidden somewhere on his body, would take him out and leave the weapons and the victory for Mekkis.

'All right,' he said to Gus. 'A unit of twenty-five creeches and their full war equipment will be placed at your disposal. Use them with wisdom.'

As Gus, amazed at his own success, turned to go, Mekkis called after him, 'But if you come across something called a Nowhere Girl, destroy him, her or it immediately.'

'Yes sir,' Gus said, and saluted.

'What's wrong?' demanded Ed Newkom anxiously.

Paul Rivers, lying on the couch in the fortune-telling parlour, with the telepathic amplifier on his head, had abruptly tensed with agitation. 'My God,' he said, but he had become so absorbed in the thoughts which he received that he sounded, not like himself, but like Percy X. 'She's screaming!'

'What are they doing to her?' Ed asked.

A long silence followed. Outside, afternoon hung heavily. Ionocraft horns beeped. A churchbell tolled five o'clock, and a slight breeze moved the curtain at the window. 'She's in a restraining jacket,' Paul said at last, again in Percy X's voice. 'She's lying on a table with wheels, going down a long, unlit hallway.' A pause; then he spoke again, this time, eerily, in the voice of Joan Hiashi. 'Damn it, Balkani, this is absurd! Let me go!'

Ed leaned forward moistening his lips nervously. Now what's happening?'

'She's in a room with padded walls,' Paul answered, again in Percy X's voice. Time passed and then he spoke again. Using the voice of Rudolph Balkani. 'Robots one and two—take her out of the restraining jacket.' Then again in Joan's voice. 'Stop that. No! I won't let you! It's no use struggling, Miss Hiashi; these robots are at least ten times as strong as you are. That's it. You see, it's much easier when you cooperate. I'm not going to hurt you. After all, I am a doctor, Miss Hiashi. You're certainly not the first unclad woman I've ever seen. Now, please, slip into this. No, I won't!' The voices ebbed back and forth, as if tugging each other, conflicting in a counterpoint, with each struggling for dominance.

Ed Newkom listened with repugnance, almost unable to believe what he saw and heard; the personality of Paul Rivers had vanished completely.

Doctor Rudolph Balkani handed Joan Hiashi what looked to her like a pair of loose-fitting coveralls made from black plastic. She put them on and one of the robots zipped her up from the back. Only her head remained showing, she discovered. The coveralls had been lined on the inside with some material so soft that she could hardly feel it.

'You are no doubt familiar, Miss Hiashi,' Balkani said, 'with the practices of certain mystic hermits; I refer specifically to the practice of sensory withdrawal. We possess now, thanks to contemporary science, an improved version of the hermit's cave. It is called the sensory withdrawal tank.' He pressed a button and a sliding panel opened in the floor to reveal a pool of dark, still water. Balkani picked up a helmet with no windows in it.

'The most successful method of sense withdrawal is an immersion tank where the subject floats on water at blood temperature, with sound and light absent. When you put on this helmet and are lowered into the pool you will see nothing, smell nothing, touch nothing and, thanks to the sensory blocking drug with which we have injected in you, there will not remain even the experience of your body, its pains and motions and chemical alterations. Put on the helmet, Miss Hiashi.'

She did not. The robots, however, did it for her.

Seemingly calm now, Joan said to Balkani, 'Have you ever been in the tank yourself?'

'Not yet,' Balkani answered. At his command the two robots lowered her into the pool, uncoiling the air-hose that led to the helmet; watching, Balkani lit his pipe and puffed on it thoughtfully. 'Give my regards to oblivion, Miss Hiashi,' he said softly.

A knock sounded on the door. Rudolph Balkani glanced up from his notebook, frowning, then ordered one of his robots to open the door. His superior, Major Ringdahl, stepped into the room, his eyes alert.

'Is she still in the tank?' Ringdahl inquired.

Wordlessly Balkani gestured towards the dark pool in the floor. The major peered down and saw the top of Joan Hiashi's helmet just breaking the surface and her body, distorted by ripples, floating motionless under the water. 'Not so loud,' Balkani whispered.

'How long has she been in?'

Balkani examined his wristwatch. 'About five and a half hours.'

'She's so still; is she asleep, Doctor?'

'No.' Balkani removed the pair of headphones he had been wearing, detached one and handed it to Major Ringdahl.

'Sounds like she's talking in her sleep,' Ringdahl said, after listening intently. 'Can't make out what she's saying, though.'

'She's not asleep,' Balkani repeated; he pointed to a rotating drum lodged within a bank of instruments: tiny pens traced irregular lines on graph paper. 'Her brain wave pattern indicates exceptional activity, almost at the satori level.'

'The satori level?'

'That's the state in which the barrier between the conscious and subconscious mind disappears; the focal point of consciousness opens out and grows tenuous and the entire mind functions as a unit, rather than being broken up into a multitude of secondary functional entities.'

Ringdahl said, 'Is she suffering?'

'Why do you ask that?' The question surprised him.

'I believe that Percy X is continually following her thoughts. If he sees that she's going through a period of discomfort maybe it'll put a little more pressure on him to listen to our side of the story.'

'I thought you wanted a cure,' Balkani snapped. 'I'm a doctor, not a torturer!'

'Answer my question,' Ringdahl snapped. 'Is she suffering or not?'

'She may have been for a while. In a certain sense she passed through the experience of losing the outside world and then her body—an experience a great deal like death. Now, however, I would venture to say that she's happy. Perhaps really happy for the first time in her life.'

Space did not exist.

Time did not exist.

Because Joan Hiashi had vanished; no infinitely small point where space and time could reintersect remained. And yet the work of the mind continued. The memory still maintained itself. The near-perfect computers wandered over the problems which they had been studying before, even though a great many of these problems had become phrased in such a way as to be unsolvable. The emotions came and departed, though the earlier dizzy pendulum-swing between anguish and ecstasy had now ceased almost completely. Here and there a ghostly semi-personality half-formed, then faded out again. Her rôles in life hung empty in the simplicity of her mind, like costumes in a deserted theatre. It had become night on the stage of the world and only one bank of work-lights remained on, dimly illuminating the canvas-and-sticks flats that only a short time earlier had stood for reality.

Balkani had been right, or at least half right. Happiness did exist here, the greatest happiness possible for a human being.

Unfortunately, no one remained to enjoy it.

8

Robots lifted Joan gently from the pool and laid her with infinite care on a table nearby. Removing her helmet Balkani said, 'Hello, Miss Hiashi.'

'Hello, Doctor.' Her voice echoed as if far away and he recognised the sound; after the therapy this often came about, this dreamlike aspect of speech and mentation.

'Looks like she's in a trance,' Ringdahl said prosaically. 'Let me see if she will react to a direct command.'

'If you must, go ahead,' Balkani said with irritation; he felt irked that his unprofessional military superior had intervened at this crucial stage.

'Miss Hiashi,' Ringdahl said, in what he obviously hoped constituted a properly hypnotic voice. 'You are going to sleep, sleep, sleep. You're falling into a deep trance.'

'Am I?' The girl's voice lacked any trace of emotion. Ringdahl said, 'I am your friend. Do you understand that?'

'Every living being is my friend,' Joan answered in the same far-distant voice.

'What's she mean by that?' Ringdahl asked Balkani.

'They often come up out of extended sense-deprivation spouting nonsense,' Balkani answered. 'And she won't do anything you tell her to, either. So you might as well not waste your valuable time.'

'But she's hypnotised, isn't she?' the major demanded with exasperation; clearly he did not understand.

Before Balkani could reply Joan spoke again. 'It is you who are hypnotised.'

'Snap her out of it,' Ringdahl growled. 'She gives me the creeps.'

'I can't snap her out of anything,' Balkani said with a slight ironic smile; he felt mildly amused. 'She's as wide awake as we are, if not more so.'

'Are you just going to leave her like that?'

'Don't worry.' Balkani patted his military superior patronisingly on the shoulder. 'She'll return to normal in a few hours all by herself, if she wants to.'

'If she wants to?' Clearly Ringdahl did not like the sound of *that*.

'She may decide she wants to stay this way.' Balkani turned and spoke softly to Joan. 'Who are you, dear?'

'I am you,' she answered promptly.

Ringdahl cursed. 'Kill her or cure her, Balkani, but don't leave her like this.'

'There is no death,' Joan said, mostly to herself. She did not really seem inclined to communicate; she seemed, in fact, virtually unaware of the two of them.

'Listen, Balkani,' Ringdahl said angrily. 'I thought you said you could cure her of political maladjustment. Now she's worse than ever. Let me remind you that . . .'

'Major Ringdahl, allow me to remind you of three things. One, that I did not promise anything. Two, that the treatments have hardly begun. And three, that you are meddling where you lack the specialised training to know what you're doing.'

Ringdahl had raised his finger skyward to make an angry pronouncement, but forgot what he intended to say when Joan sat up suddenly and said, in the same detached voice, 'I'm hungry.'

'Would you like a meal served in your room?' Balkani asked her, feeling sudden sympathy for her.

'Oh yes,' she said expressionlessly, then reached back

and unzipped her cellophane coveralls. She slipped out of them without the slightest trace of embarrassment, but Major Ringdahl turned a mottled red and glanced the other way. Balkani watched her dress, a strange pain in his chest; it was a new feeling to him, one which he had never in his life felt before. Her body seemed so small and childlike and helpless; he wanted to protect her, to help her stay in her waking dream where everyone was her friend and death did not exist.

Joan led the way out of the room, a slight smile on her face, like a Mona Lisa or a Buddha, and as she passed Balkani he reached out and touched her arm. As if she had become a saint.

After she had eaten, Joan Hiashi moved to the window of her cell and looked out. The sun had sunk low; evening lay ahead and very close. Autumn came early here, and a leaf, its rusty red made all the more brilliant by the sun, hung from its branch a few feet from Joan's barred window, twisting meagrely in the breeze. Joan studied the leaf.

The sun disappeared.

The leaf became a black silhouette against the fading sky, and stars appeared behind it, faint but distinct. The smell of the sea hung in the air, and the taste of salt.

Joan continued to watch the leaf while the breeze grew colder and stronger, rising and falling with a great rushing sound, like someone breathing in her ear. Still she stood motionless, one hand resting on the smooth sill of the window, the other by her side.

Still she watched the leaf as the last fragments of daylight departed and the wind, growing stronger with each moment, rushed in her face and played in her hair.

An hour passed.

Two.

The leaf danced wildly to unheard music, tossing, twisting, swirling its cape in the darkness, seeming to sense that it had an audience.

At midnight Joan was still standing there, watching the leaf.

All night long she watched, and all night long the leaf danced for her with frantic abandon in the gale.

At dawn the wind slackened and the leaf drooped.

One brief weary turn, like a bow, and it fell, zigzagging downward to lose itself in the multitude of other leaves on the ground below. Joan's eyes followed it, then lost it. The sun came up.

Joan sighed. She suddenly realised that she felt cold. Her skin had turned blue and was covered with goosebumps. Her teeth began to chatter and she shivered and rubbed herself vigorously, trying to get warm. Joan Hiashi had returned to normality, if by normality one meant this leafless world in which humans normally live.

Percy X stared stupidly at his bandaged left hand. He had cut it himself, smashed a drinking glass and attacked himself with one of the fragments; the sharp pain had dragged him back from that sucking void into which he had followed Joan, the void that drew her in and had almost drawn him in after her. He had realised with sudden terror that his whole personality had begun dissolving, evaporating, and he had tried to break his telepathic contact with her but had been unable to, at least not until he had cut himself.

Now he cautiously entered her mind again—and found himself a stranger there. Everything had been moved about. He withdrew again, icy sweat breaking out on his forehead.

All at once he sensed someone coming. Guards.

The door unlocked and opened; one of the guards leaned in and said in a bored voice, 'Come along now, buddy. Make it fast.'

Presently, with a guard on each side, he made his way briskly down a long corridor, past endless processions of locked doors. *I wonder where they're taking me,* he mused—and scanned their minds to find out. They were taking him to Joan, on orders from Balkani. But why had Balkani given such orders? On a whim, most likely; on a drug-induced impulse. Still, Percy felt uneasy. Even Balkani's whims seemed to have some enigmatic, almost unnatural, purpose.

To his amazement he found the door to her cell unlocked; in fact it hung slightly ajar.

'A visitor for you, Miss Hiashi,' one of the guards announced.

Joan, who had been lying on her bunk gazing blankly at the ceiling, sat up and smiled. 'Hello, Percy.'

The change in her could be seen at once. A certain air of seriousness, of maturity, that he had never perceived before. The guard closed the door, leaving the two of them alone.

'You look like a sleepwalker,' he said presently.

'I'm awake for the first time in my life. Sit down. I have something to say to you.'

Cautiously, he seated himself at the foot of the bunk.

Joan said, 'I have always told everyone, including myself, that the thing that came first with me was my career in TV. But that was a lie, even though it was a lie I convinced myself I believed in. There have been times when I've told myself I was in love with one man or another. You, for one. But that wasn't true either. I threw away my career when I went into the mountains

86

looking for you, and I've goofed up every love affair I've ever had, one way or another. Time and again, when success in one project or another was almost in my possession, I did some damn fool thing that ruined everything for me. Now I know that the one thing I've always feared most, deep down inside, was to succeed, to get the things I thought I wanted. I've always thought that people were against me, or that I had bad luck, but my real enemy was me. All my life, whenever I've tried to get something, the same demonic figure has stepped into my path and commanded me to halt, the same relentless phantom with my face. Doctor Balkani gave me a knife and let me kill that phantom. She screamed, Percy; she screamed for hours as I slowly cut her to pieces, as I washed myself clean of her. Now she's dead and if I feel anything for her it's a kind of loneliness. I'm all alone now that Joan Hiashi is dead.'

'You're psychotic,' Percy said sharply. 'Because of the suffering you underwent; I know: I stayed in contact with you.'

'I'm not insane, Percy. And Balkani is only helping me to find what I've always wanted, all that time I pretended I wanted fame and prestige and money and you. He's given me the courage to see . . .'

'He's given you mental and spiritual death.'

'Oblivion,' Joan said.

'Can't you see what he's done to you?'

'Who, God?' Joan asked in a far-away voice.

'No, Balkani!'

'Doctor Balkani is my friend. If I have an enemy it must be God.'

He grabbed her by the arm, yanked her towards him. 'I know what you experienced; don't you understand? Because of my talent I was there in the water and silence with you—you're not telling me anything I didn't go through *myself*. What I'm telling you is that . . .' He broke off, tried to think it out. 'You felt love for me; I did also, for you. What wasn't real about that?' He clutched her arm, squeezing fiercely. 'Answer me . . .'

'What do you see,' Joan said, 'when you look at me?' A little Japanese doll; isn't that right? I don't blame you for that. I gave myself to you for a plaything and you played with me. What could be more natural? But I'm more than a doll. I really am tall, Percy; tall as a mountain. I'm tired of hunching down.'

'Nobody is asking you to hunch down.' He tightened his grip on her arm.

'You're a telepath; you read men's minds. But you don't understand them. Doctor Balkani does not read minds, but he understands completely. How do you explain that, Percy X? I know why it is.' She smiled her strange, distant smile. 'Balkani has read one mind down to its darkest depths. *His own mind*. Because he understands himself completely he doesn't need telepathy to understand others. Don't be fooled by the fact that he takes drugs; if you saw yourself the way you really are, as he sees himself, you'd need drugs, too, to stand it. You might even kill yourself. Because we are all monsters, Percy. Demons from hell—foul, filthy, perverted and evil.' She spoke these words calmly, without a particle of emotion.

Percy said, 'Stop talking like that.'

Carefully, she removed Percy X's hands from her arm. 'From now on I say what I wish. I've spoken to you honestly for the first time and you've acted as if I were insane; psychotic, as you put it. Okay. I expected that. I see that in order to be clear I must also be cruel.

I've been trying to explain, all this time, that I don't need you any more, Percy. Or anyone else.'

Late at night, after the last customer had left the fortune-telling parlour, Paul Rivers and Ed Newkom opened the crates which had arrived by rocket freight earlier in the day.

'Weapons, eh?' Ed said with satisfaction. 'Something to fight our way into Balkani's . . .'

'Not exactly,' Paul Rivers said, removing armfuls of plastic-foam padding from the foremost crate.

A robot lay in the crate. And, in the other crate there would be a second robot. Both based on prototypes which Balkani himself had designed during the war. *And now remodelled,* Paul Rivers said to himself, *to serve my own purposes.*

'And what's this?' Ed demanded. 'A high-frequency transmitter?'

'No, a sensory distorter.' This, too, had been one of Balkani's inventions, dating back to the pre-war Bureau of Psychedelic Research. 'We'll test these items out tonight, to make certain they work. Then contact Percy X and spring him as soon as we can.'

Dawn had almost come when Percy X, lying sleepless on his cot in his cell, heard the voice of Paul Rivers speak within his mind. 'Tomorrow, Percy.'

But how? Percy thought.

Quickly and without wasting words, Paul outlined his plan. It impressed Percy X, impressed him very much.

'Now I'm going to bed and try to get a few hours' sleep,' Paul Rivers telepathed. 'And I advise you to do the same. I'll see you tomorrow, if nothing goes wrong.'

Percy felt the amplified mind of Doctor Paul Rivers

switch off, leaving only a last fleeting impression of great weariness.

Sleep. That was easy enough to say, Percy thought, but not so easy to achieve. Something lay in the back of his mind, something which ate away at him without let-up, draining away his strength and resolution slowly and steadily. He wondered what it was.

A picture of Balkani's face rose in Percy X's mind. The beard. The pipe. The fire-ignited glittering eyes with the dilated pupils. *No matter who rules this planet,* Percy realised, *Balkani will still find a place in the ruling class. . . . And what about me?* he asked himself. *What in God's name is happening back in Tennessee? What are my last Neeg-parts doing? Assuming any are left . . .*

I've got to get out of here, he said to himself. *If I stay, Balkani will have me the way he has Joan. . . . Only a matter of time,* he realised. *And, when that happens, it'll be foreordained as far as the bale is concerned.*

He would not be getting any sleep, not with such thoughts lodged starkly in his mind.

At dawn the garbage truck came crashing and banging down the old highway beside the fjord and halted at the guard station just before the bridge, as it had done so many times over the years. The guards gave it a routine inspection and let it by. The truck crossed the single-span suspension bridge and made its way, roaring, snorting and wheezing, up the road to the gates of the prison. There it was again inspected and again passed, to park at last behind the prisoners' mess hall. Two men in white coveralls stepped out, marched over to the garbage shed and disappeared inside, a moment later two guards stepped out into the sunlight and made their way briskly down the hallways that led from the kitchen.

A clank of keys sounded at the lock of Percy X's door and a voice said, 'Routine check. Step outside a minute, will you?' Percy scanned the area telepathically. Nobody was anywhere near.

He looked in the direction of the voice. There stood a man in a guard's uniform. It was Percy X.

For a moment the human Percy X and the robot Percy X gazed at each other; then the human stepped out into the hall, where no TV spy-monitors watched. A moment later the robot Percy X re-entered the room and lay down on the cot, while the human Percy X, now dressed in the guard's uniform, locked the door.

Quickly he made his way to Joan Hiashi's cell, making use of the knowledge of the combination on the intervening doors that he had gained in his protracted period of mind-picking.

Two Joan Hiashi's stood outside Joan's door, one in prison uniform, the other in guard's uniform. He could not tell which one was the robot and which the human until the one in the guard's uniform said, barely audibly, 'She says she won't go, sir.'

'If you don't go,' Percy whispered hoarsely to her, 'I won't go.'

For a moment Joan remained silent. But he read in her mind, *I can't have you giving your life for me.* She shrugged, then, and began listlessly, with agonising slowness, to change clothes with the robot.

A moment later two 'guards', one tall and one short, made their way to the garbage shed. After a pause two garbage men, one tall and one short, emerged from the shed and carried two garbage cans to the truck. The shorter one seemed hardly strong enough for the task, but somehow she made it. Two more trips and all the garbage had been taken out.

The white-coveralled figures climbed into the truck and drove back out to the gate.

'Took a long time, today,' the uniformed inspector at the gate said sourly.

'Had to stop by the men's room,' Percy X said.

The inspector shrugged and waved them past.

'Why didn't they recognise us?' Joan whispered.

'Look at me,' Percy said briefly. She looked—and her eyes widened, The man beside her wasn't Percy X at all. 'It's these gadgets on our belts,' Percy explained. 'They project a false image into people's minds; they make us look like what the person expects. Balkani perfected it a number of years ago, according to Doctor Rivers.'

'Oh yes,' Joan said faintly. 'Doctor Rivers. I wondered when he'd show up again.'

They passed inspection at the other end of the bridge, too, and from there they found themselves in the clear.

In a garage just off the fjord-side highway, Doctor Paul Rivers and Ed Newkom sat on the fender of a sleek ionocraft, tensely waiting. Next to the wall two authentic garbage men, stiff and silent, looked sightlessly on.

'Yes,' Paul said, glancing with approval at the hypnotised men. 'I haven't lost it, the ability.' In the old days, at the beginning of his professional practice, he had gone in a great deal for hypnotherapy . . . as had Freud. *Much better,* he reflected, *to save something of the potency of hypnotism for special occasions.* Such as this.

'Got a light?' Ed asked taughtly.

'I don't smoke,' Paul answered. He brought out a tin of Inchkenneth Dean Swift snuff. 'Oral gratification is oral gratification, and snuff doesn't get soot down into your windpipe.'

'I'll use the car lighter,' Ed muttered, with a psychosomatic cough. 'Snuff—keerist; I prefer a bag of peanuts.' He climbed into the ionocraft and nervously lit a cigarette.

For a time the two men sat in silence, one smoking and the other taking pinch after pinch of snuff, and then they heard the distant roar of the elderly garbage truck, slamming and banging down the highway.

Instantly Paul hopped down from the fender and swung open the garage door. With a snort and noisy backfire the truck came rumbling in and stopped with a squeal of brakes. Percy X killed the turbine and jumped out, followed, more slowly, by Joan Hiashi. Paul at once closed the garage doors and strode over to greet them.

'I'm Paul Rivers, Percy,' he said as he shook hands with the hard-eyed Neeg-part leader, 'and this is my co-worker and friend, Ed Newkom. Perhaps you recall, Miss Hiashi, that we met. Briefly.'

Joan gazed at him with unfocused eyes and expressionless face, saying nothing. Within him, Paul shuddered. *What has Balkani done to her?* he asked himself. *Such a lovely little creature and he's managed to turn her into—God knows what. But,* he thought, *perhaps I can help her.*

He gave a few instructions to the hypnotised garbage men, then stood back with a humourless smile on his lips as they obediently climbed into their truck. 'Open the garage door for them,' he said to Percy X. 'Before they break it down.' Percy opened the door; the truck motor exploded into life and, a moment later, lurched down the short driveway, swerved out onto the highway and headed off in the direction of Oslo.

'Let's get out of here,' Ed said impatiently, stubbing out his cigarette. The four of them got into the ionocraft,

Paul seating himself behind the wheel; with a whoosh the vehicle shot out of the garage and over the smooth waters of the fjord.

'There's one thing I'd like to know, Doctor Rivers,' Percy X said, not using his telepathic powers out of politeness to the non-telepaths present. 'Why did you go to such risk and trouble to get us out?' He felt suspicion, deep and abiding.

'We have a favour,' Paul Rivers said, 'to ask of you.' His voice held softness—and yet it sounded peculiarly firm.

'What favour?'

Paul Rivers said, 'We want you to go back to Tennessee and die. Preferably like a hero.'

9

Major Ringdahl met Doctor Rudolph Balkani in the dim hallway outside the psychiatrist's office. Balkani tried to get by him with only a mumbled greeting, but the major touched his arm and said, 'Wait a moment, there.'

Fidgeting impatiently, Balkani waited.

'I understand you're now working with both Joan Hiashi and Percy X, Doctor,' Ringdahl regarded him acutely. 'How's it going?'

'Not too well.' Balkani frowned as he stroked his irregular beard. 'I think I may be pressing them too hard. Their reactions have become almost—mechanical.'

The major slapped Balkani on the back, an apparently friendly gesture . . . but Balkani felt the pressure of force beneath it. 'Keep at them; they'll crack sooner or later. After all, they're only human.'

When he finally managed to break free of his superior, Balkani found himself thoroughly depressed. The thing that annoyed him most seemed to be Ringdahl's insistence that he 'crack them'. *I want to cure them, not crack them,* he thought to himself as he entered his office.

He thought, then, about Joan Hiashi. An interesting case but not in accord with any of his previous findings; her reaction to oblivion therapy was unique. He would have to write an entire new chapter in his thesis on the New Psychoanalysis, all because of her. *Perhaps,* he reflected, *I'll have to revise my entire theory. What a painful thought . . . a life's work down the drain, just because of one exception.* And yet, as he well knew, a single inordinate exception such as this did not prove the rule; it *broke* the rule.

At this point he had completed half of the crucial last chapter. He could not finish it until he had closed the Joan Hiashi case, one way or the other. *Perhaps,* he mused, *I'll honour her by naming a mental illness after her.* 'The Hiashi Complex.' No, that was perhaps too ambitious. 'The Hiashi Syndrome.' That would be better.

Closing the door of his office after him he seated himself at the foot of his analyst's couch and glared sightlessly at the rather tarnished bust of Sigmund Freud looming on top of his bookcase. *Quite a frowning father figure, aren't you?* he thought.

Joan Hiashi was late. What kind of idiots did they have for guards, anyway? They were probably making time with her this very moment, the animals, pawing her with their sweaty soldier hands. He got irritably to his feet, paced back and forth a few times, then sat down again and reached for his pipe.

Footsteps in the hall. He leaped back up to his feet, spilling tobacco from his pouch; this he did not notice, because the door had begun to open. And there she stood.

'Hello, Doctor.' She entered the office, behind her the guard shut the door. As on every other occasion of late she seemed cool and remote, even indifferent. 'What do we do today?' she asked as she slipped noiselessly into a chair facing him.

'The tank,' Balkani said. 'Or some multiphasic profile tests. Or perhaps just a little chat, eh? We ought to get to know each other better.'

'Anything you say, Doctor.'

If only she would react emotionally to him in some way. But she never seemed even to hate him, let alone show any affection. He said, for a trial start, 'Why don't you call me Rudolph?'

'Anything you say, Rudolph.'

'That's better.' But it was not better; as with every previous response it had an empty, listless quality to it. 'Perhaps a little dip in the sensory-withdrawal tank would be nice today,' he decided. 'What do you think about that?'

'Anything you say, Rudolph.' She began dutifully to undress; Balkani watched, his palms sweating. In a moment she stood nude before him, waiting for his next command.

He picked up the diving coveralls from their hook on the wall and walked hesitantly up to her. 'Can I help you?' he said hoarsely.

'Anything you say, Rudolph.'

With trembling fingers he helped her into the garment,

96

then, just before he zipped her up the back he kissed the nape of her neck, quickly and furtively. Then he led her by the hand to the tank chamber.

As the two robots lowered her into the water he looked again at the strangely mechanical patterns made by her encephalic waves on the polygraph. So unusual; unique, in fact. Unlike anything he had ever come across before. And he did not like it, not at all.

But there seemed to be nothing he could do about it; for reasons which he did not comprehend, the situation had got out of hand.

Paul Rivers guided the ionocraft so low that the ancient and obsolete telephone wires still used in the bale of Tennessee shot past above him. *There's no alarm out for us,* he reflected. *But still, as we near the mountains, it's best that we don't attract any undue attention from wik radar stations.*

The lights on the vehicle had been turned off, except for the infrared headlights; Paul wore conversion goggles so that he could get a look at the countryside for some distance ahead—without being seen. A low overcast hung everywhere. It depressed him.

Because of the low altitude he had slowed to less than a hundred miles an hour, feeling little danger of pursuit; it therefore came as a very disagreeable surprise when the radio, which had been tuned to the local police band, suddenly sprang to life long enough to announce curtly, 'Unidentified ionocraft in sector C, heading south without lights. This is police central. Repeat: unidentified ionocraft in sector C; move to intercept. May be trying to join the Neeg-parts.'

'Get out the laser rifles,' Paul said quietly. Percy X and Ed Newkom moved quickly to obey. Joan continued to stare out into the darkness, seemingly indifferent to the danger.

He lifted the craft to a slightly higher altitude and increased the speed to a hundred-and-fifty, then two hundred miles an hour. Yet he had it still only a little above treetop level; it seemed wiser to him to hug the earth as long as he knew that the police did not have a positive fix on him. Glancing at his own radar he saw that two fast craft hung behind and above him, catching up fast. *They'll probably try to take us alive to begin with,* he decided. 'Two police vehicles approaching from the rear,' he informed Percy X.

'I can see their running lights,' the Neeg-part leader said, lifting his laser rifle to his shoulder as he stood beside the open hatch, coils of wind flapping his clothes.

'Think you can nail both of them before they have a chance to launch anything at us?' Paul asked.

'Sure,' Percy X said, and fired two short bursts. Behind them one of the police craft exploded; the other zigzagged a moment, then plunged earthward like a streamlined brick and buried itself in a hillside.

Paul changed course, changed course again, then increased speed to a dangerous three hundred miles per hour. Trees now whipped past too fast to dodge if he should come upon a really tall one.

Now the radio blurted out, 'Unidentified ionocraft definitely enemy; just shot down two of our patrol crafts. All crafts converge on sector G. Shoot to kill.'

There's one nice aspect to consider, Paul said to himself. *At least it can't get any worse.*

But he was wrong.

At that instant, out of the darkness ahead appeared a high-tension power line. At the speed which he was travelling Paul did not have a chance to react to, let alone dodge, the oncoming obstacle; he could only hang on as the ionocraft struck the wires with an impact that smashed his head forward against the wheel, almost knocking him unconscious. But, though his mentation had become dazed and confused, the habit-patterns imprinted in his subconscious by years of flying high-velocity ionocrafts under all sorts of conditions remained functioning; he fought frantically to regain control as the vehicle spun wildly and lost altitude. Another crash shuddered through him as the ship struck the top of a sandy hill and bounced once again into the air.

Now, miraculously, Paul managed to get the ship under control and, still swerving erratically, to regain a little altitude. He glanced briefly at Joan, Ed and Percy X. All seemed stunned, perhaps unconscious. The ion grids of the ship had suffered severe damage and threatened to break off at any moment; the ship appeared to be losing power. He realised with reluctance that he would be able to keep it in the air only a few minutes more. *I guess*, he thought bitterly, *we'll have to get out and walk*.

Just then the radio spewed forth another message. 'Unidentified ionocraft surrounded! Close in, all patrol craft, and shoot on sight!'

'It has become time,' said the Timekeeper, to key into the Common Mind broadcast from the home world, sir.' The nervous little creech gestured towards the surge-gate amplifier in the corner of the Administrator's office.

'Eh?' muttered Mekkis in response.

'Sir, this is the third time this month that you have failed to join the fusion. How will you know what is happening back home?'

'I have more important matters to attend to. Anyhow

I know what is occurring back home. My enemies are enjoying themselves at my expense. Why should I plug in just to empathise with their gloating?'

The Oracle chimed in gloomily. 'It is not from the home world that the darkness approaches.'

The Timekeeper slunk off in silence and Mekkis returned to his 'more important matters.' This consisted of a reading of the entire published works of the brilliant but verbose Terran psychiatrist, Doctor Rudolph Balkani; Mekkis had secured microfilm copies of all the books available through the channels of the Bureau of Cultural Control and had devoted virtually his complete attention to them. Never before had he encountered a thinker that so obsessed him. The very first sentence of the initial book had passed through him like a shot.

'The number of men on this planet is great but finite. The number of potential men within men is infinite. I am therefore, greater than the entire human race.'

This thought would never have occurred to a being accustomed to the telepathic melting together of the Great Common, and yet there was something about it, a certain incredible yet plausible egotism, a fantastic daring that seemed to speak to a deep, hitherto untouched part of Mekkis' spiritual mind. It seemed somehow to explain the painful state of affairs existing between himself and the other members of the Ganymedian ruling class. *They all, every last one*, he thought, *are against me; yet I know I am right—that in fact I've been right all along. How can such a condition occur unless Balkani is correct; unless one being really can be greater than the entire race from which it comes?*

Balkani's method struck him as outrageous. Instead of performing systematic experiments, cautiously moving the boundary of knowledge forward inch by inch,

Balkani simply looked within his own unique mind and described what he saw, brushing aside whole schools of psychiatry with a single snide remark, making not even a feeble attempt at politeness, let alone scientific fairness. Yet his theories produced results. Balkani, the master, lurched drunkenly into the unknown, carelessly tossing off dogmatic statements as if they were proven facts simply because they seemed to him, intuitively, to be true. Then others could follow behind him, picking up his ideas and testing them scientifically, and produce miracles.

A method of training latent telepathic ability that really worked.

A type of psychotherapy that seemed to be a brutal, all-out attack on the patient's ego, yet which cured in weeks supposedly impossible-to-cure mental illnesses such as drug addiction and far-advanced schizophrenia.

An electromagnetic theory of mind function that opened the way for partial or complete control of the mind by electromagnetic fields.

A way of measuring the presence of Synchronicity generated by schizophrenics—an acausal force which, by altering consistently the patterns of probability, made the objective world appear to collaborate with the psychotic in the creation of the half-real world in which his worst fears would, against impossible odds, come true.

Was it these results that impressed Mekkis, or was it the example of Balkani the man? The latter. Mekkis had begun to see himself in the Terran psychiatrist, feeling at one with this man who had set himself up in opposition to his entire race.

It would be interesting, Mekkis mused, *if I turned into a Ganymedian Doctor Balkani.*

Glancing up for a moment he discovered that one of his wik secretaries had been typing, for almost a minute now, to attract his attention. 'Gus Swenesgard is here, Mr Administrator,' the secretary declared.

'I haven't time to see him. What does he want? Did he say?'

'He wishes more fighting units in his Neeg hunt in the mountains. He claims he can clean out the whole lot of them if he just has a little Gany first line hardware.'

He did not want to think about the Neegs; he was struggling to understand a particularly fine point in the illogical logic of Dr Balkani's 'Centrepoint, Action at a Distance and ESP.' Aloud he said, 'Give him what he wants. Keep an eye on him, though. And don't bother me about it.'

'But . . .'

'That is all.' Mekkis flicked the switch with his tongue, the switch that turned the microfilm viewer to the next frame.

With a shrug the wik departed. Mekkis instantly forgot the exchange as he buried himself once again in the twilight world of 'Centrepoint Paraphysics.'

When Gus Swenesgard heard the Administrator's decision, as relayed to him by the wik secretary, he said rapidly, 'Mekkis says I get anything I want?'

'That's correct,' the secretary said.

'First off,' Gus said with an expansive smile. 'I'd like all the Gany fighting units in the bale transferred to my command. Then . . .' He pondered a moment dreamily. '. . . I'd like to do a little reorganisation in the governmental structure.'

'Who do you think you are?' the wik secretary said dryly.

Gus chuckled, slapping the somewhat annoyed secretary on the back. 'I'm the Kingfish around here now, sir. That's who I am.' He then left the Gany HQ building. Whistling contentedly; he knew exactly what he had— for reasons unknown to him—achieved.

There, up ahead, Paul Rivers made out a highway, and on the highway a huge trailer truck zoomed through the night. He hauled back gently on the controls of the iono-craft and thought, *Why not?* The craft responded slug-gishly . . . but he found himself swinging down behind the truck, approaching it, as he intended, from the rear.

Now, he said to himself, and cut the grids. On the last dying power he sailed in through the open upper half of the trailer and settled on its cargo with a crash. The driver spun around, startled, and gazed back through his cab window as Paul took aim with a very mean-looking laser rifle. 'Keep driving,' Paul said, over the roar of the truck engine.

'You're the boss, man,' the driver said with a sheepish grin; he turned his eyes back on the road. *He must think,* Paul realised, *that we're hi-jackers; the first chance he gets he'll try to signal the law.* And the law, of course, would be here in a second.

The driver, however, appeared to be a Negro. Percy.' Paul Rivers said urgently. 'Pull yourself together and tell the driver who we are. Quick!'

Beside him Percy blinked, then read Paul's mind and the driver's with two swift probes, then yelled at the driver, 'Hey, dad, you know who I am?'

The driver, studying his rearview mirror, said, 'Yeah, I know who you are; I do believe you're Percy X. I would have joined you in the hills except I got a wife and kids to think about; I gotta stick around and keep them from killing each other.' He laughed. Mockingly.

'You going anywhere near Gus Swenesgard's plantation?' Paul asked. *We're headed,* he thought hopefully, *in the right direction.*

'Goin' through the northern end,' the driver answered.

'Fine,' Percy X said, with palpable relief. 'From there I'll be able to get back to my men on my own.' To Paul he said, 'Are you coming with me?'

Paul glanced at Joan Hiashi and said, 'No. Ed and I will be parting company with you there.'

'You want to take Joan with you?'

'She'll be safer with me.'

'Nobody is safe nowhere these days,' Percy X said bitingly.

'Do you want her to stay the way Balkani has made her?'

After a pause Percy X said, 'You'll keep me posted on how she's doing? With that amplifier of yours?'

Just then an ionocraft whooshed overhead, then another and another. 'Where'd they go?' demanded a voice on the police radio. 'They've vanished!'

Another radio voice crackled out with resignation. 'The Neegs have those new weapons. I heard about it on TV; they can make themselves invisible.'

Paul Rivers could not resist smiling faintly when he heard one of the police mutter under his breath, 'Never can find a Neeg when you really want one.'

10

It had been a long climb up to the mountain cave where the most enigmatic of the weapons captured by the Neegparts from Gus Swenesgard's excavation had been hidden. Everyone felt acutely tired.

Percy X, seated in the shade, examined a manual which had come with a rather ordinary-looking device, something which resembled a high-frequency oscillator. 'Look at this,' he said to a group of his men who lounged near him, staring absently into space.

The 'parts passed the manual back and forth, examining it; then one of them said, 'Doctor Balkani.'

Lincoln strolled up and dropped languidly to sprawl beside Percy X; he took the manual and leafed through it. 'I didn't want to use this baby,' he said. 'There seems to be a good reason why it wasn't used during the war.'

'Those white worm-kissers might have thought it was a good reason,' Percy said broodingly; he wiped sweat from his forehead with the back of his arm.

'Maybe, maybe,' Lincoln said, taking off his battered horn-rimmed glasses and gesturing nervously with them. 'I might agree with you about the other gadgets we got in this haul. They've turned out to be useful—but a little scary.'

'Scary?' Percy said with annoyance.

'Well, you know, these constructs are supposed to produce illusions.' Lincoln frowned. *'But there's something wrong.* Did you ever see an illusion that left footprints? That could kill a man?'

'No,' Percy said. 'And I never will.'

'That's what you think. I tell you, man, there's something about these weapons that just isn't right; you use one, just once, and you are never quite the same again. You begin to wonder what's real and what isn't, or if anything is real.'

'But you've been using them anyway, right?' Percy said.

'All but this baby; this is something else. The manual says it never got tested, that it *couldn't* be tested. Nobody, not even the guy who built it, knows exactly what it'll do, but from the looks of what the other constructs do . . .'

'If I have to use it,' Percy said grimly, 'I'll use it. There's no such thing as a weapon that's too powerful.' *Even*, he thought, *if it's one of Balkani's inventions.*

It took a while for good-natured, doddering old Doc Burns to locate, by X-ray, the instant kill device which the Gany technicians had inserted under the skin of Gus Swenesgard's arm. But once it had been found, it was quite easily removed.

'That sure is a load off my mind,' Gus said, lighting a cheap grocery-store cigar and inspecting the organic bandage on his arm with interest. 'You're sure there isn't another one of those little fellers on me somewhere?'

'Not a chance,' Doc Burns declared as he placed his operating tools in the steriliser and turned on the heat.

Gus took a long drag on his cigar, trying, without consciously being aware of it, to drown out the hospital smell, the smell of disinfectant that permeated the atmosphere of Doc Burns' operating room. 'You know, Doc,' Gus said thoughtfully, 'you may not know it but you are looking at a rising star in the political firmament.'

'Hmm,' Doc Burns said.

106

'That's right, sir.' Having the instant kill remote control device removed had given him the powerful expansive feeling. 'Take it from me; that worm administrator has got himself all wrapped up in book reading, and he don't pay no attention to what's going on in this bale. You know who is running things around here?'

'Who?' Doc Burns said, humouring Gus.

'Me,' Gus said with satisfaction. 'That's who. And I got big plans. What would you say if I told you I wasn't going to root out those Neegs? What if I told you I was going to make a deal with 'em?'

'I'd say you were out of your ever-loving blue-eyed pea-pickin' mind,' Doc Burns said laconically.

'Listen, Doc. Those Neegs got hold of some gadgets they stole from me, real strange doodads left over from the war, and they been doing something with them, but those Neegs are too ignorant to know it but with hardware like that they just might be able to really give those Gany worms something to think about. Maybe they just might be able to take Earth back from them. And, Doc, the man who controls those weapons will be the man who controls this planet.'

'You just mind your own business, Gus. Don't get too big for your breeches.'

'Don't get nowhere without taking risks,' Gus said, slapping him on the back.

A half hour later Gus sat rocking himself in the shack of one of his trusted Toms, a blaring transistor in his hand.

'Don't mind the music,' Gus said. 'It's just to cover up our voices in case this little house of yours happens to be bugged or somebody happens to be covering it with a long-range listening snout.'

'What do you want to talk about that has to be so

107

secret, Mr Swenesgard?' Little Joe asked, a short, thin Tom; a good Tom who 'knew his place'.

'I want you to go up to the hills, Little Joe,' Gus said, placing a fatherly hand on the Negro's shoulder.

'Me? Go up there with those wild men?'

'I want you to talk to whoever is in charge up there, now that the Gany worms have got Percy X. I want you to tell them I'd like to make a deal with them. Tell them I intend to join forces with them—with me, of course, in charge, but them forming maybe a sort of council to back me up. Tell 'em I think—Christ, I *know*—we can lick the Ganymedians. With my leadership and their weapons and troops.'

'Do I have to do it, Mr Swenesgard?' Little Joe's voice shook.

'Yes, you got to do it,' Gus said emphatically.

'Okay, Mr Swenesgard. I guess I'll go right ahead and do it next week for sure.'

'Not next week, Joe.'

'Tomorrow?'

'Today, Little Joe. Right now.'

'Well, okay, Mr Swenesgard. If you say so.' Little Joe nodded miserably.

In the front room of Dr Rudolph Balkani's apartment near Oslo, Norway, Major Ringdahl paced restlessly. 'You worked on some sort of electronic mind-warping device for the UN, didn't you?' he said.

'It was a good weapon,' Balkani said. 'Too good; they couldn't use it.'

Ringdahl said, 'It seems that shortly before we captured Percy X his followers got their hands on this hell-weapon; it had been buried in Tennessee, near the Smoky Mountains. The Gany Great Common is worried about it. What, specifically, does this weapon accomplish?'

'The result of its operation is peculiar. Each person continues to perceive reality, but it comes to him as a hallucination, a private vision which can't be related to the shared vocabulary of images. From this arises a swiftly-developing encapsulation. The person affected is not, strictly speaking, isolated; he experiences the "real world", but he cannot make head nor tail of it. The delightful aspect of this mechanism is that it attacks only the percept-portion of the neurological structure; cognition, the functioning of the frontal lobe, continues unimpaired. The victim can still *think* clearly; it is just that now the data received by the undamaged higher brain centres cannot be fathomed or made into . . .' Balkani rambled on and on; history, however, does not record the rest of his tirade. Winded at last, Balkani paused to take a pill from the square, silver pill-box which he carried in his vest pocket.

'You say,' Ringdahl said, 'that the operator of this weapon is as much impaired as . . .'

'The basic quality of a weapon,' Balkani said, 'is not that it destroys but that it acts to defend its owner. With this item the operator becomes as disoriented as the target-individual. It functions through the centre-point at which all minds in a given Synchronity field are connected; therefore it would very likely take out every thinking being on this planet, and probably all those on Ganymede as well, since they have telepathic representatives here.'

Ringdahl said, 'The Neegs might not mind the suicidal aspects of this hell-weapon.'

Smiling, Balkani selected another pill—at random— from his chaste and ornate pill-box.

109

Snow yet remaining.

The mountain slopes in haze. Evening.

Such stillness. The cries of crickets sank into the rocks. On a withered branch a crow alighted, peered down into the long grass and weeds. The breeze ruffled his feathers but still he sat, silent and watching, as the light of day slowly faded.

In the grass something flowed, seemingly black in the dimness. It flowed slowly, draining into the dust. It was blood.

A dead man lay there, half-hidden in the weeds, waiting to be found the following morning. A thin short dead Negro man, face down, spread-eagled in the weeds, naked. Little Joe.

On his back, carved with laser beams, carved in cooked flesh and drying blood, a message to Gus:

WE DON'T NEED YOU, WHITE MAN

11

'Neeg-parts proceeding through pine forest, grid line 27-39,' said the tracking turret mechanically. 'About seven of them. Confirm, seven.'

Gus, riding in the lead ionocraft of a wing of ten autonomic ionocraft scout-bombers, said into his microphone, 'Keep low, out of direct line-of-sight of the target area.'

The other crafts responded with curt affirmations.

They must be getting careless now that Percy X isn't around to babysit them, Gus reflected. Coming out in broad daylight. Now that was really dumb. 'Surround them,' Gus said into the microphone. 'I want you to spread out and when you're in position let me know. But make sure to stay at treetop level. And keep plenty of cover between you and them.' *After all,* he reflected, *they have those weapons.*

The ten scout-bombers split up, each swinging off in a different direction. Gus brought his own craft to a hover on the opposite side of the ridge from the detected Neeg-parts. *With surprise on my side,* Gus said to himself, *I'll have an easy kill. Pay back those bastards for what they did to Little Joe.*

The whoosh of the supporting downdraft through the ionocraft grids sounded so faintly that Gus could make out the calls of birds in the forest around and just below him. He hoped the Neegs didn't have the modern detection instruments needed to hear that faint whoosh, to separate it from the common wind noises of the mountain afternoon. It did not seem likely that they did.

The craft being on full automatic, Gus had nothing to do but lean back and sun himself, meanwhile smoking and daydreaming. *One way or another,* he said to himself, *Gus Swenesgard is going to the top. And I mean the top.* To succeed in wiping out the Neeg-parts where the Ganys themselves had failed . . . that alone was enough to make him the most likely choice for top position in the bale—or maybe even something higher than that. Why not head wik of the whole North American continent?

He began, in his mind, to compose the expostulation which he would make to Mekkis once the Neegs had finally been pacified. *I'm a man of the people,* Gus said to his imaginary Gany audience. *The common man will see himself in me, identify with my aims. It'll make*

111

*people more peacable, seeing a poor slob like themselves
on the top of the heap.*

That wasn't quite right. But something like it—and
Gus had plenty of time. The Neeg-parts were still alive
and kicking; this, of course, was only temporary. However, one had to consider it.

At that moment the signals which he had anticipated
began to float in from the other ships; when he received
notice that they had all reached their positions he said
into his mike, 'Okay; hit 'em hard!' He then signalled
his own craft to rise up above the brow of the ridge, so
that he could watch; he had no intention of risking his
own neck by joining in the attack. As he cleared the crest
he saw the other scout-bombers sweep in from all direc-
tions to converge on a spot a mile away. Expectantly,
Gus waited for the bomb burst.

But no bomb burst came.

'What's wrong?' Gus demanded into his mike.

The squeaky voice of a creech responded, 'They're
gone!'

'What do you mean?' Gus said, glancing hurriedly at
the detection gear. 'I'm still picking them up from here!'
But now a strange and fuzzy sensation filtered over his
mind; when it had passed he looked again at the detection gear—and sure enough: no trace remained of the
Neeg-parts. 'What's going on here?' he demanded, a
note of panic in his voice.

As he stared fixedly in the direction of the converging,
now aimlessly milling ionocrafts, he saw something else.
Something far worse. An eye. A huge unwinking eye in
the side of the mountain. Watching him. And then the
mountain began to move, like a living thing. It raised a
vast arm, an octopus pseudopodium, and smashed two
of the ionocraft bombers with a single whip-like motion.

As he turned his own ionocraft and fled back over the brow of the hill he had, for an instant, the distinct impression that someone was sitting in the empty seat next to him. Percy X. Laughing.

'I'm sick,' the Oracle said.

'I ask you for a forcast,' Mekkis said contemptuously, 'and all you can say is, "I'm sick".'

'I don't want to look in the future,' said the creech. 'Looking at the future is what makes me sick.'

Mekkis did not feel too well himself. *Perhaps,* he thought, *I've been reading too much. Yet I can't stop now; somewhere in these fantastic theories of Balkani's is the answer. The more I read the more I become convinced of it.*

The concept of selective awareness, for example. That could explain so much of what seems paradoxical about these reports we've been getting about illusions that seem real. The mind selects, out of a mass of sense data, those ones of all the possible items to pay attention to, to react to, to treat as 'real'. But who knows what the mind may be rejecting, what lies unseen out there in the world? Perhaps these illusions are not illusions at all, but real things that ordinarily are filtered out of the stream of incoming sense data by our intellectual demand for a logical and consistent world. Why were they unable, previously, to hurt us? Because, quite literally, what we don't know can't hurt us. Being unknown to us . . .

Doctor Balkani!

Mekkis stared in amazement at the figure of the bearded, intense-looking man sitting in the chair across from him, smoking a pipe. As the Gany Administrator watched, the figure faded and was gone.

113

Shaking his entire body in a tic-like whipping motion, Mekkis said to himself, *I must go on. Time is growing short.*

'Snap out of it, man,' Percy commanded one of his troops who seemed to have given in, for the moment, to hysteria.

'But I tell you I'm still invisible!' shouted the man.

'I turned off the projector an hour ago,' Percy said, leaning against a tree with studied casualness. 'You can't be still invisible. I can see you as plain as day.'

'But I can't see me!' shouted the distraught Neeg-part. 'I hold up my hand in front of my face and, man, there ain't nothing there!'

'Hey, Lincoln,' Percy said, turning to his second-in-command. 'You see that man standing there, don't you?'

'Sure I do,' Lincoln said, squinting through his scratched and broken horn-rimmed glasses.

'Anybody here who can't see this man?' Percy demanded, turning to the rest of his troops which sat and stood in a loose semicircle around him.

'We all see him okay,' they murmured.

The Neeg-part leader turned again to the 'invisible' man. 'Now pick up your projector and let's march.'

'No, man. I ain't never going to touch one of those things again. Not to save my life.'

'Are you defying my orders?' Percy picked up his laser rifle.

'Easy does it, Percy,' Lincoln said, gently pushing the rifle to one side. 'I'll carry his projector.'

Percy hesitated, then shrugged and let Lincoln have his way.

At nightfall they reached one of their forward dugouts and there counted noses. The man who had imagined himself to be invisible was no longer with them.

'He really did disappear,' one of the men said.

'No, he didn't,' Lincoln said. 'He just left the party and headed for Gus Swenesgard's plantation.'

'What?' Percy shouted. 'And you just stood there and let him go? If you knew he was a deserter, why didn't you shoot him?'

'You can't shoot everybody, Percy,' Lincoln said grimly. 'And since you've started using those illusion projectors quite a few men have gone over the hill . . . and if you don't stop, a lot more will follow.'

'I can't stop,' Percy said. 'With these weapons I can finally really make a dent in those stinking wiks; I can really hurt them. Without these weapons it would only be a matter of time before we'd be finished.'

'Then,' Lincoln said stoically, 'you'd better use them full-force and use them now. While you still have a man or two left.'

The defectors drifted into Gus Swenesgard's plantation by ones and twos at first, then in larger groups. Gus, suspecting some trick, had the first ones shot, but then, when he began to understand what was going on, started routing them into a hastily-constructed prison compound and set about personally interrogating them in the lobby of his hotel.

One fact became clear almost from the outset. Every one of the defectors was at least somewhat mentally disturbed—some seeming to be full-blown hallucinating paranoid schizophrenics.

Their most frequent delusion was that Percy X had not been captured but still led them, up in the mountains, or that he had escaped by some miracle and returned to them. Just to make sure, Gus phoned Oslo and talked directly to Dr Balkani; the psychiatrist assured him that both Percy X and Joan Hiashi remained safely under lock and key.

'Just wishful thinking,' Gus muttered as he hung up the phone.

The other delusions were remarkable for their variety and lack of consistent pattern. If one could speak of a 'typical' case one might take Jeff Berner, a one-time captain in Percy's rag-tag army, as representative.

Gus did not need to be a mind reader to tell instantly, when Jeff was brought into the lobby for questioning, that here stood a very, very scared Neeg.

'You Jeff Berner?' Gus asked, lighting a cigar and settling back comfortably in an overstuffed chair. Jeff, of course remained standing.

'That's right.' The unhappy black man nodded.

'That's right, *sir*,' Gus corrected sternly. *You don't get nowhere with these Ubangis*, he said to himself, *unless you get them to show you the proper respect*.

'Sir,' Jeff said lamely.

'Now tell me; what made you leave the Neeg-parts?'

The ex-Neeg-part shifted nervously from one foot to the other and answered, 'them thought projectors. They did things to my mind.'

'What kind of things?' Gus made his voice kind and sympathetic; the best results came from treating Neegs as the simple children they were. *Let them look on me*, Gus said to himself, *as a sort of father*.

'Well, any kind. You turn on the machine, imagine something, and what you imagine, well, it seems to sort of come true. Only—sometimes, when you turn off the machine, the illusion doesn't go away. You go on seeing it . . . maybe for days.'

116

'And in your case what did you imagine?' This was the part of the interviews which Gus had come to enjoy the most. Each story seemed more grotesque than the last.

'Well, sir,' began the Neeg uncertainly, 'it began when me and two other troops made a little raid for supplies and food, on a home on the outskirts of your plantation. We were having a hard time, see, because they, the farmer and his wife and two sons, they were keeping us off with lasers, and we thought that your troops would be on us in a few minutes with ionocrafts, so I figured I'd rustle up some reinforcements with the illusion machine, just a few extra men to throw a scare into the farmer. Well, the gadget zapped up twenty-four men and they all fought like veterans, then helped us to carry the supplies we captured up into the mountains. That was fine, I guess, except I don't see how an illusion can lift a boxful of real canned food. The catch was that when I turned off the gadget the twenty-four men didn't go away. They stayed with me in the hills and ate like horses, sir, like horses. But I didn't mind. I kind of got to liking one of the guys. He was a real pal; we used to spend hours talking, and he seemed to know all kinds of things. Never met such a smart fella in all my born days. Mike Monk was his name, and he had been borned and raised in New York. Said he joined Percy X because he had a hard time getting a job, which was sort of a joke, but has some truth in it. Lots of men joined Percy because nobody else wanted them.

'Once he saved my life. Shot down a homotropic dart that acted like it had my name on it. After that I stopped thinking he was just an illusion. I just took it for granted that he was real. Well, one night we were in a dugout talking when I suddenly realised that the other

117

twenty-three men were gone. I said, "Hey, Mike, what's happening, man?" and he said, "Nothin', Jeff baby"; only I happened to notice that Mike didn't have any feet. I said, "Hey, Mike, what happened to your feet?" and he said, "My feet are okay, man", only then I sort of realised that I could see through his legs. "Hey, man," I said, "you know something? I can see through your legs," and he said, "How you talk, man," and I said "Hey, where did you really come from?" and he said "Like I told you; I'm just a simple New York cat"; only I could see his legs were gone and I could see through all the rest of him, so I said, "Hey, man, where you going to?" and he said, "I ain't going nowhere. I'm going to stick with you." His voice was getting kind of faint and far-away so, I yelled, "Hey, where are you?" and I heard him say, so faint I could hardly hear it, "Right where I always was and always will be, standing by your ever-loving side," and poof, he was gone. I never seen him since.'

'And then,' Gus said, 'you defected?'

'No,' Jeff said. 'That came later, after I used the illusion machine again.'

'What did you use it for the second time?' Gus asked, fascinated.

'Why, what would you do with a thing like that if you was in my shoes, Mr Swenesgard, sir? I made me a pretty little girl friend with it!'

'Then after the girl friend started to fade out . . .'

'No, sir. Before the girl friend started to fade out. I tell you, sir, that little girl was the meanest, most complainin' woman I ever did see! I'm no coward but, sir, that little girl went ahead and chased me right out of the Neeg-parts.'

In a cave high in the mountains a figure lying in a sleeping bag stirred, sat up. 'Lincoln,' Percy grated harshly, reaching out a hand to shake his sleeping comrade.

'Huh?' muttered Lincoln, 'whazat?'

'I've made up my mind,' Percy said. 'We've been on the defensive long enough. With the hardware we have now we stand a real chance to go on the offensive, to bust out of these mountains and really kill a few wiks.'

'I've been thinking the same thing, Lincoln said sleepily. 'As far as these weapons go we've hardly scratched the surface.'

'Pass the word along. We want all the new weapons in action, except that Big Daddy up at Summit Cave. I got to admit, goddam it, man, that that thing scares me, even me. I'll leave one day for preparation, then we hit Swenesgard with everything we've got. If we can take his plantation we'll have all the first-line Gany hardware he's got on loan from the worms, and plenty of Toms who'll come over to our side when they see we're winning.

'With a little bit of luck we might even be able to step on that worm, Mekkis. From what I hear through the network Mekkis doesn't do anything but lie around reading. He leaves all the work of running the bale of Tennessee to Swenesgard. When we take the plantation we'll have to keep going, spreading out as fast as we can, so that if the Gany military starts hitting with nuclear missiles we won't be all bunched up in one place. Everything depends on speed. And,' he finished, half to himself, 'on illusion.'

'The Nowhere Girl is coming!' wailed the Oracle.

'Don't shout at me like that,' Mekkis snapped. 'Can't you see I'm trying to read?' *All is illusion,* he said to himself. *Each of us is a windowless monad, without any*

119

real contact with a world outside ourselves. Balkani proves it. Why therefore should I concern myself with meaningless phantoms such as Nowhere Girls and Neeg-parts and the Great Common? The world is a picture and if I wanted to change it, all I would need to do is imagine it to be different.

For instance, if I cared to I could imagine an earth-quake and . . .

A vast tumbling-motion spilled through the room around him, a wave rolling through him and past, leaving a yawning fissure in the floor.

Mekkis gazed down at it with satisfaction while the Oracle babbled meaninglessly, hysterically.

Gus learned about Percy's planned attack from a defector—two hours before sundown on the night of the attack. He drove at once to the office of Administrator Mekkis and asked to see him.

'Mr Mekkis,' the wik secretary said with obvious relish, 'has left word he does not want to be disturbed. Under any circumstances.'

'The Neeg-parts are attacking in force tonight,' Gus said; he sweated visibly, even though the waiting room in which he stood was air-conditioned.

'Is that all?' the secretary said scornfully. 'The Neeg-parts are always attacking something or other. Surely you can handle it.'

Gus opened and closed his mouth, turned red and then, without another word, turned and stomped out. Once in his ionocraft he took firm hold of the micro-phone, lifted it to his lips and began rapidly to issue orders.

Within an hour the assorted forces of Gus Swenesgard, made up of everything from small nuclear missile launchers to Toms with pitchforks, moved in a jumble of confusion toward the great black shapes that now, in the moonless night, could be seen thundering and rumbling towards them.

The nuclear missiles were fired before the forces met, but they did not go off. The vast rolling masses of blackness seemed to swallow them up. Then the ionocraft scout bombers swept in, and they, too, disappeared.

Gus sat in his ionocraft, hovering over his plantation, and watched what took place through a bank of small TV monitors, mounted on the control panel, which received signals from various units of his motley army. One screen in particular caught his attention; it displayed a transmission from a squad of creech-operated ionocrafts that had moved nearer the enemy than any other of Gus' units. There on the screen Gus saw, forming out of the blackness, a herd of gigantic African aardvarks as big as dinosaurs with evil, glittering eyes, huge claws and ears like circus tents, and with unbelievably long tongues that lashed out and licked ionocrafts out of the sky.

'Oh my God,' Gus said, unable to accept the fantastic sight. 'Not aardvarks!'

In the wake of the stampeding aardvarks came a battered autonomic ionocraft taxi bearing Percy X and Lincoln Shaw. 'You see that?' Percy yelled. 'I'll bet they didn't expect that.'

'It's wild,' Lincoln said, more awestruck than enthusiastic.

'What else can you do?' asked the taxi.

'How about something really beautiful?' Percy shouted. 'How about a gigantic bird all made of flame? How about a phoenix?'

'Okay,' Lincoln said. 'One phoenix coming up.' He

adjusted the controls on the construct in his lap and concentrated. Out of the clouds of dust that rose in the wake of the aardvarks formed an incredible winged creature, more than a thousand feet in wingspread. It seemed to be made up of burning light or perhaps electricity, and all the colours of the spectrum flickered chaotically over its feathered surfaces. Its eyes consisted of points of blindingly bright blue-white light, like twin welding torches, and, as it glided majestically ahead of them, it left in the air a trail of sparks like falling stars. The two men in the ionocraft could smell the ozone caused by its electrical fire, and the wind from its wings blew the ionocraft roughly about, almost overturning it. Now and then it opened its blazing beak and uttered a hoarse cry that sounded, to Lincoln, like the scream of an ignorant and innocent thing being tortured to death.

'Isn't it great?' Percy yelled.

'*De gustibus non disputandum est,*' the taxi said philosophically.

'Charge!' shouted General Robert E. Lee as he galloped into battle at the head of a troop of mounted Valkyrie. Their long blond hair streamed in the wind as they screamed ancient runic oaths and trampled beneath the hooves of their ice cream white horses creech, white and Tom, without discrimination.

A squadron of vampires dripping blood from their fangs and wearing the insignia of Baron Manfred von Richthofen's Flying Circus flapped by overhead, while Samson, hair and all, strode past, swinging the jawbone of a duckbill platypus.

Through the milling confusion rushed a battalion of Brownie Scouts, cracking skulls right and left with overbaked cookies, while a kosher butcher, with his vorpal meat cleaver, reduced the enemy to meat knish. Red-assed baboons charged in behind him, pushing super-market carts armed with fifty calibre maching guns. A rock-and-roll group headed by a young long-hair trum-peter named Gabriel played the 'jerk' while a team of trained surgeons removed one appendix after another, throwing in an occasional lobotomy to avoid monotony.

Four squealing transvestites in silk evening gowns swung, with deadly accuracy, blue sequined purses filled with cement, while cavemen and Pygmies hurled pois-oned confetti.

A dayglow orange unicorn reared up with seven soldiers impaled on his horn like so many unpaid bills, and a man-eating plant with an Oxford accent sucked dry one spinal column after another with a sound like a rude boy trying to suck up the last drop of a milkshake. Sadistic peacocks circulated among the wounded, tick-ling to death the unwary with their feathers. A pregnant ten-year-old teeny-bopper, smashed on acid, mercilessly beat all comers at chess, passing the time between moves by painting pictures of her favourite celebrities, Marshal Ky, Marshal Koli and Adolf Hitler, on her naked but flat chest, with purple lipstick.

Little nude lesbians no more than one inch high scampered over the faces of the enemy removing beards one hair at a time. The Wolfman chewed contentedly on a big toe, spitting out the toenail. A brave band of lawnmowers and growling laundromat machines exe-cuted a brilliant flanking movement and attacked from the rear. Everywhere the air was filled with the ghastly sound of guttural shrieks, whoops, howls, oily laughter, gasps, grunts, lisps, drawls, yells, croaks, bellows, whines, sensual moans, brays, yaps, meows, tweets, bleats, roars and maundering.

But at the moment when it appeared as if the ordinary forces of Gus Swenesgard would be wiped out to a man, the fantastic hordes of Percy X began to quarrel among themselves. Frankenstein attacked the Wolfman. Godzilla attacked King Kong. The Boy Scouts criminally assaulted Girl Scouts.

The sabre-tooth tiger was blinded by the needles of shoe-making elves. A spikelet of Meadow Fescue (festuca elatior) was struck down by a cowardly blow from Bucky Bug, anthers, pistil, paleae, glume and all. Suddenly it became a free-for-all. Every apparition for himself.

In an instant Percy realised that if he remained in the midst of the nightmare battle just a moment too long, he and his men would fall victim to their own phantasmagoria. In fact at this very moment a carnivorous vacuum cleaner was attempting to break into the taxi in which he and Lincoln Shaw sat.

'Retreat!' Percy shouted into his mike. 'Back to the mountains before it's too late.'

At dawn the battlefield lay silent.

A mist hung over the scene, hiding the incredible carnage left behind by the night's orgy of destruction. As the sun rose higher in the sky the mist began to evaporate, and with it the multitude of fantastic shapes and forms which the mist had hidden. Ghostly dead elephants and ruined tanks melted together, became translucent, then transparent, then faded away. Heaps of corpses, wearing the uniforms of every age and nation, blurred and shimmered and became one with the fog. Ionocraft and creeches and Toms and Neeg-parts . . . they, too, faded and turned to a fog, the real and the unreal meeting and blending and then vanishing together.

124

By noon the mist and what the mist had hidden had both disappeared without a remnant, and in the shuddering midday heat nothing remained but weeds and the bent, upward-poking stalks of grass.

12

Paul Rivers did not face the man; instead he stood gazing out of the hotel room window at the seamy side of Knoxville, Tennessee, as it baked in the afternoon heat. *Everything he says is true,* Paul thought to himself. *And yet . . .*

'There are only two possible outcomes to the situation up there in the hills,' Dr Martin Choate, Paul's immediate superior in the World Psychiatric Association, said. 'Percy will not use the hell-weapon, and he will lose his pelt and the ego of the human race will be lost with him, or Percy will use the hell-weapon and that will be the end for all of us. Don't you see that?'

Paul did not speak; he only nodded. *Yes,* he thought, *I see that. But I can't accept it.*

'Then you must also see,' Dr Choate, said, 'that we have no choice but to kill him and to burn his body, making it look as if he died in action—heroically. Our organisation has already begun to make its move. Seven high-ranking wik officials have already killed themselves under hypnotic suggestions implanted by their psychotherapists. Other more complex plans have already been set in motion, but we must have a martyr; we must have our John Brown, our crucified Christ, if we hope to gain the support of the broad masses of people. *Isn't the freedom of the human race more important to you than the life of one man, one murderous fanatic?'*

Paul said, 'Why me?'

'Because he trusts you. You saved him from Balkani. We don't have anyone else who could get near him.'

'That's the problem,' Paul said. 'He trusts me. That's why I can't do it.'

'He won't be able to probe you telepathically. We can hypnotically implant a cover story in your mind, a story you'll believe yourself until the moment comes to strike. He'll never know.'

But, Paul thought, *I'll know*. 'I've got to have time to think,' he said aloud.

Choate hesitated, then said, 'All right. We can let you have a few days.'

They shook hands and Dr Choate left without a backward glance. *Everybody says 'we' these days*, Paul thought absently. *Nobody says 'I'. Everyone represents some formless, irresponsible group and nobody represents themselves.*

Stepping out of the bedroom, Joan Hiashi said, 'I want some growing things.' She smiled at him uncertainly. 'May I?'

'Okay,' he answered, and then experienced a sudden upsurge of spirit, a sudden sense of freedom. 'Let's go out and buy up a whole garden.'

Ed Newkom met them in the hall as they were going out. 'What's up?' he asked, surveying their faces.

'We're going to do a little shopping,' Paul said; he glanced over his shoulder and saw Ed gazing after them in bewilderment. It was Dr Rivers who thought with pleased satisfaction, *Joan is showing no signs of returning to the world of common experience. She wants some-*

126

thing. It was, however, just plain Paul who, as he and Joan emerged from the hotel entrance, glanced up at a white cumulous cloud that towered like a god over the dirty slum and thought, *Beautiful, beautiful, beautiful.*

'Joan?' Dr Balkani said.

'Yes, Rudolph,' said the robot Joan Hiashi, sitting on the analyst's couch in Balkani's poorly-lit office. Every day contained the same elements, now; Balkani could see no more change in his patient than he could in his massive bronze bust of Sigmund Freud. Except that sometimes he received the impression that the bust smiled at him. It was in no respects a pleasant smile.

Balkani said, 'Joan, is there anything you want?'

'No, Rudolph.'

Eyeing her, he said, 'Then you must be happy. Are you happy?'

'I don't know, Rudolph.'

'You are,' he said. Puffing angrily on his pipe, he paced the floor. Joan did not follow him with her eyes; she continued to stare straight ahead. Abruptly he stopped pacing; he seated himself beside the robot and put his arms around it. 'What would you do if I kissed you?' he said. It did not respond. 'Put your arms around me,' he barked at it, and it obeyed. He kissed its lips for a lengthy time, but it was boring; up on his feet again he said, 'That was boring!'

'Yes, Rudolph.'

'Take off your clothes!'

The robot disrobed, quickly and without wasted motion. Balkani also disrobed, almost falling on his face when he got his feet caught in his pants.

'All right, now kiss me again.'

They kissed again.

127

After a few moments Balkani shouted, 'It's still boring!' He pushed her roughly down on the couch and kissed her one more time, but it was still boring. Untangling himself from the robot's arms he sat with his back to her at the foot of the couch. He felt old. *Why do I love her so much?* he asked himself. *I never loved anybody so much.* Getting to his feet he rummaged in his clothing until he found his pill-box; opening it he shook out all the pills, the entire assortment of all colours and shapes—without water he gulped them down. 'You see?' he said to the robot Joan. 'I don't care whether I live or die. And neither do you; right?'

'Yes, Rudolph.' Tonelessly she spoke, as before. Emptily.

'There's one emotion I'll bet you can still feel, *Fear.*' He lurched over to the bookcase and, with a harsh, laboured grunt, hauled down the bust of Freud. 'I'm going to kill you. Don't you even care about that?'

'No, Rudolph.'

Balkani, in anguish and fury, lifted the massive bronze bust high over his head; he moved back towards the couch. She did not flinch; she did not, in fact, even seem to notice. He brought the bust down on her skull with all his strength. Her cranium burst.

'I only meant to . . .' he began numbly as the robot Joan Hiashi slid from the couch and fell, sprawling, onto the floor. And then he saw within her head—not formless organic tissue—but a crumpled turret of printed microminiaturised circuits and solid-state cerebro-spinal axis components, as well as delicate sweep-range surge gates, low-temp liquid helium battery conduits, homeostatic switches—with portions of the circuitry grotesquely still functioning, including the standard feedback networks for the master turret which, though it hung out of

128

her skull and dangled down her cheek, continued ticking like some debrained reflex-arc crayfish-thing. And he recognised the handiwork which had gone into the building of the thing as his own.

'Joan . . . ?' he whispered.

'Yes, Rudolph?' answered the robot faintly, and then its power failed.

'Joan?' Paul Rivers said.

Sitting on the bed of their Knoxville hotel room, in the hot red light of sunset, Joan Hiashi said, 'Yes, Paul.'

'Is there anything you want?'

'No, Paul.' She studied the windowbox that now rested just inside the window of their room, and at the tropical plants that grew there. Then she smiled, and Paul Rivers smiled, too.

The therapy may be slightly unorthodox, he reflected, *but it's working. Now if she can only start caring about —not only plants—but people and the world of a common, shared reality.*

'They want you to kill Percy X, don't they?' she said. 'I overheard. I wanted to hear.'

He said, 'That's right.' And did not look at her directly.

'Are you going to do it?' she asked, without emotion.

'I don't know.' He hesitated, then said, 'What do you think I should do?' *A new twist*, he thought acridly; *the doctor asking the patient for advice.*

'Be happy,' Joan said. Getting up, she walked over to her newly purchased windowbox of plants, where she knelt and played in the dirt with her fingers. 'All these political movements and philosophies and ideals, all these wars—only illusions. Don't trouble your inner peace; there's no right and wrong, no win or lose.

There're only individual men and each one is com-pletely—completely!—alone. Learn to be alone; watch a bird fly without telling anyone about it or even storing it up to tell someone about it in the future.' She turned towards him, her voice low and intense. 'Let your life remain the secret it is. Don't read the homeopapers; don't watch the newscasts on TV. Don't . . .'

Escapism, he thought as he listened to the hypnotic voice. *I've got to be on my guard; it's compelling but false.* 'Okay,' he said to her, breaking into the flow of her words, 'while I sit here staring stupidly at the back of my hand, what happens to my patients? What happens to the people I could have helped?'

'They go on in their insanity, I suppose,' Joan said. 'But at least you don't join them in it.'

'You have to face reality.'

'My hand is real. It's the war that's a dream.'

'Doesn't it matter to you that the whole human race is enslaved by creatures from another planet? Doesn't it matter to you that we may soon all be dead?'

'I planned on dying sometime anyway. And when I'm dead, what'll it matter to me whether others go on living or not?'

Paul Rivers felt a wave of sick frustration sweep over him. *She's so imperturbable,* he thought feverishly, *so safe behind her schizoid defences. Behind that saintly façade. What absolute selfishness—what smug egotism.* Looking down at his hands he saw that his fists were clenched. *My god,* he thought; *what am I doing? I don't hit patients; I help them. She must be getting to me, reaching some deep well of repressed Balkani-ism within me.* Across from him he saw that she watched alertly, perceived the frustration, anger and—fear.

'You think this little war of yours is important,' she

said. 'But to me it's only a small and unimportant skirmish in a far bigger struggle.'

'What far bigger struggle?'

Wordlessly, Joan pointed to the windowbox; among her flowers, a contingent of red ants and another of black ants were engaged in a fracas. For the moment Paul gazed into the turmoil of writhing bodies and crunching mandibles—then he looked away, unable to speak. *Is it I*, he asked himself, *who's living on dreams and comforting illusions? Am I, in the end, the real escapist?*

Joan, he realised, was still watching the ants. But not with anguish; on her Buddha-like face he saw a faint, gentle smile.

Rudolph Balkani sat at his elaborate, solar-battery-powered, justifying typewriter and let the words pour from his fingers. More than two days without sleep, but what did it matter? The methamphetamine tablets in his silver pill-box would keep him going until he had finished.

Only a single light burned in the room: the unshaded bulb over the cluttered desk on which he worked. The rest of the room, including the sprawled figure of the ruined robot Joan Hiashi, lay in shadow. It seemed to him as if the single bulb held back, with steadily diminishing strength, a blackness so heavy and thick as to be almost touched.

He had locked the door; several times people had knocked on it but Balkani had told them to go away. They had. Both the intercom and the vidphone had been carefully smashed. The bust of Freud had done them in, too.

Now the bronze, frowning father-figure lay face-down on the floor, its anger spent. The time had arrived for

131

the son to create a universe. Feverishly Rudolph Balkani laboured on, giving birth in the form of a book to the new universe that would displace the universe of Freud, together with all the other universes before it. A generation of young people would take this book as their Bible in the revolution of youth against age.

As he worked he hummed a snatch of a tune, always the tune of one of the advertising jingles he had collected and studied in his early years. How much he had learned from TV commercials! While others turned down the TV set when the commercials came on, Balkani turned them up. The programmes had nothing to sell but middle-class morality, a dreary product at best, but the commercials offered a world where dreams were for sale, where youth and health came in a box, and all pain and suffering were smoothed over with long, beautiful, slow-motion hair. Avant-garde films? Balkani jeered at them. Nothing lay in the most surrealistic of them to compare with the charisma of TV commercials. The work of the dedicated shoestring movie-makers of the 'sixties and 'seventies was now mercifully forgotten, but video-tape copies of erotic soap and beer commercials from the same period now brought bids of up to two hundred UN dollars from collectors.

At this moment Balkani stood ready to finish his masterpiece, *Oblivion Therapy*. Why not? The Joan Hiashi case, the one remaining piece in the cosmic crossword puzzle, had fallen in—in an unexpected way, to be sure—in place. All alone in his office, Balkani laughed aloud. How simple it had become, after all. A gigantic shaggy dog story, where the whole point of the joke consisted in the fact that no point existed.

What lay behind it all?

Oblivion.

Suddenly Balkani stopped. The last sentence which he had typed had a ring of finality to it. Yes, he had written the concluding sentence of this, his life's magnum opus. Carefully he removed the sheet from the typewriter and placed it with the rest of the manuscript; he then wrapped the manuscript with care and precision and addressed it to his New York publisher. He placed the package in the outgoing mail tray and the autonomic mechanism of the tray at once whisked it from the room. So that was that.

Shuffling wearily, he made his way over to the ample medical supply cabinet, feeling at last the effects of so much lack of sleep. An overdose of quindine, he said to himself as he lifted out the hypodermic; that should provide the necessary cardiac arrest.

With a grunt, he sat down at the foot of his analyst's couch, rolled up his sleeve and gave himself the injection. His arm, from so many previous injections, had become insensitive; he felt nothing.

The needle broke as it fell to the floor from his suddenly stiffening fingers, and, with a sigh, he slid back onto the couch.

His subordinates were so much afraid of him that they did not break in and find his body until a day and a half later.

13

'What do you mean, you don't know where he is?' Dr Choate demanded.

'Just what I said,' answered Ed Newkom, shrugging his shoulders. The two men faced each other for a moment in silence in the little Knoxville hotel room and then Dr Choate turned away.

'He must have left some indication of how he could be reached,' Choate said.

'Nope,' Ed Newkom said flatly.

'And he took the girl, Joan Hiashi, with him?'

'That's right, Dr Choate.'

It had become hot in the hotel room. Choate brought out an Irish linen handkerchief and mopped the perspiration from his forehead; he squinted at the bright sunlight streaming in from the window and felt angry and irritable. 'I have to locate him; I have to know whether he plans to undertake the Percy X mission or not. It's been five days; he may be gone for good.' *Defected,* he thought, *or just plain copped out.*

'You don't know Paul very well, do you?' Ed Newkom said.

'That's the trouble; I do know him. I know how involved he gets emotionally with his patients. It's part of his style of therapy to treat the patient almost as an equal. A bad policy—it puts too much strain on the therapist. He's probably cracking up.' He felt all at once—not irritation—but genuine concern.

Paul Rivers, at that moment, knew an inner calm and peace with himself such as he had never before experienced. He had begun to learn how to do nothing. The Sexual Freedom Society had not understood how to achieve it, but Joan Hiashi did; now she was teaching him, in a run-down one-room cabin in the woods of Tennessee, a good distance from the nearest paved road. She had taught him how to lie in the sun like a vegetable—and grow roots.

Side by side the two of them lay, on the ramshackle

134

porch, only their fingertips touching. Once Paul had half-heartedly tried to kiss her, but she had pushed him gently away and he had taken 'no' for an answer. Now, after more than an hour of torpid, mindless silence, she had begun to speak, very slowly.

'I can't make love anymore; it makes me feel false, now. I'm not a woman, or a man; I'm both and neither. I'm the entire universe and just a single tiny eye, watching. To be a man or a woman is to put on an act—and I'm through with acting. It is good to touch me, though, isn't it? As it's good to touch a dog or a cat?'

'Yes,' Paul said, almost inaudibly. *This is the first time*, he thought, *that a woman has known how to let me be. How to be with me without requiring that I pay attention to her, constantly prove to her that she exists. It's true in a way*, he realised, *that being a man or a woman is, in a large measure, just an act, a certain culturally determined rôle that may have very little to do with how we really are inside. How many times*, he asked himself, *have I made love not because I wanted to but because I wanted to prove to myself and some poor woman that I was a 'real man'?*

He glanced over at Joan's expressionless profile and thought, *But she seems so far away. I wonder where she's gone, deep in her hidden depths.*

'Where are you, Joan?' he asked.

'Nowhere.'

'You're the little Nowhere Girl, aren't you?'

'You could call me that.'

A bird, probably a humming bird, caught Paul's eye; it sat on a tree-branch beyond the weed-infested yard, singing. It had one short song which it sang over and over again, always exactly the same. As Paul watched it, he could have sworn that the bird paused and looked back

135

at him, silent for a moment, and thoughtful. Man and bird contemplated each other across the expanse of undulating heat and then, abruptly, the bird resumed its singing. Suddenly, and without warning. Paul felt painful emotions rising into activity within him. Fantasies danced on his brain and unexplained tears dimmed his vision. Perhaps he had been a bird, once; perhaps this small bird had recognised him as a brother.

The bird came closer, still singing.

I have wings, too, Paul thought. *But you can't see them. And I can feel the wind under them, feel the air bearing up the weight of my body.*

When his vision cleared, the bird had gone.

'He knew you were listening,' Joan said. 'He's a terrible ham.'

'Does this sort of thing happen to you often?'

'Yes,' Joan said. 'They're all hams, the birds and animals, but they won't show off to you unless they sense that you won't hurt them. They don't have as much knowledge as humans, but much more wisdom. Some of them, particularly cats, are great philosophers and holy men.'

'Are you a holy woman?' he asked, surprised at his own question.

'Perhaps. If I have any ambition it's to be something like a saint or holy woman. What else is worthwhile?'

Paul said thoughtfully, 'You've made it about halfway.' He chose his words with care. 'Buddha and Christ began by going off into the wilderness, into the kind of aloneness you seem to be in now, *but they didn't stay there*. They came back—to try to do something for the rest of us. Maybe they failed. But at least they tried.' With a grunt he rose unsteadily to his feet, stood swaying, then stretched and felt all right.

'Where are you going?' Joan asked.

'Back to the city,' Paul said grimly. 'I've got work to do.'

Much to his own surprise, Gus Swenesgard found himself still alive after the Great Battle. And, being alive, he could indulge himself in the luxury of admiring his enemy.

'We got some pretty good Neegs in these hills,' he said to nobody in particular as he stumped through the lobby of his hotel and out into the morning sunshine. Pausing, he inhaled a good, hefty amount of dusty air laden with the healthy smell of decaying weeds; he then ran his hand over his somewhat unshaven jowls, coughed and spat. 'I gotta quit smoking one of these days,' he muttered under his breath. But he knew, deep inside, that he didn't have the strength to do it.

Instead, he pulled out a cigar and lit it.

Ah, he thought dreamily, *that's better.* There was nothing that covered up the taste of old, stale smoke quite so well as new, fresh smoke. Gus exhaled, then swaggered down the front steps—carefully avoiding the broken one—and headed for the prisoners' compound down the street; several vacant lots had been fenced in to provide a temporary dwelling-place for the Neeg-part deserters that streamed into Gus' plantation in ever-increasing numbers. Since the battle of the phantoms the trickle of turncoats had become a torrent. *If they just keep using that illusion machine*, Gus said to himself, *I'll be sittin' pretty.*

When he reached the fence of the prisoners' compound he paused a moment, pondering. *It's no good*, he decided, *keeping those good, black bucks standing around idle; I think we'd better get a little public works goin' here. First off I'll get a sign-painting factory going to make signs and posters that say 'FULL EMPLOYMENT' and 'LET'S ALL PULL TOGETHER' and that sort of thing, and then we'll have to get a money factory going to pay them. I think we got some old steel engravings of confederate money in the museum that are still as good as in the old days when Jeff Davis lived.*

Once we get the money printed up, he thought happily, *we can start fixin' up this place. Roads to be built, ionocrafts to be repaired. And a government to be set up.* In his mind he began to list all his relatives and personal friends; they, of course, would have to have special political positions set up for them . . . and under them he would create an overlapping maze of job-holding bureaucratic functionaries whose tasks would be vague—but who would constitute all the good people personally familiar to him on a man-to-man hand-shaking basis throughout the bale. *Have to get a few of the right kind of Neegs in there, too,* he reflected. *To keep them from getting restless.*

He spotted the lean, stooped figure of Doc Burns emerging from the compound, past the guards. 'How's it going, Doc?' Gus said.

'You ought to get these people out of here; these conditions breed disease.'

'How about sending them into battle—they left the 'parts; now let them fight the 'parts.'

Doc Burns said, 'These Neegs didn't leave the 'parts; they left those weapons. And they're not about to go into battle against those same weapons. It was bad enough for them, being on the giving end; they're not about to . . .'

'But,' Gus said, 'I gotta clean out those hills once and for all. I haven't given up; I *can't* give up.'

138

'Use robots.'

'You know, Doc, maybe you got something there.' *A robot army*, Gus thought, *might not be affected by illusions*. Anyhow it seemed worth a try. 'An all-out offensive against the Neeg-parts,' he said aloud, 'using nothing but automatic and homeostatic weapons.'

Doc Burns said sceptically, 'Where will you get such weapons?'

'From the worms,' Gus said. 'I'll get Mekkis to give me the best they've got; stuff maybe which we've never seen.' He strode off.

'Read no more,' the Oracle pleaded mournfully. 'The hour of the Nowhere Girl is upon us!'

Mekkis wove, sent out his tongue to depress a button on his office intercom. 'Send in the Huckster,' he ordered his wik secretary.

A moment later the door slid aside; a smiling well-dressed Terran with bow tie and purple velvet coveralls entered. 'I am the Huckster,' he informed Mekkis.

'I know,' Mekkis said, and he thought, *You must be a telepath, too; otherwise you never would have learned to scramble. And also*, he said to himself, *you must be a graduate of Balkani's school.*

'You are, I understand,' the Huckster said, 'looking for certain documents, certain obscure papers written by Dr Rudolph Balkani and circulated privately to students at his seminars. Papers crucial to a comprehension of Balkani's theories, yet withheld from the general public.'

'Do you have such papers?'

'For a price.'

'Of course,' Mekkis said. 'I'm told that it is you who sold my predecessor, Marshal Koli, this vast collection

139

of plastic model planes and other various historical odds and ends now enshrined in these offices. If you can supply me with these documents I will trade you the entire World War One sequence of fighter aircraft for them.'

'You've got to be kidding,' the Huckster said, grinning.

'I realise that you may find my generosity a little overwhelming,' Mekkis said, 'but we Ganymedians are a . . .'

'You don't understand.' The Huckster had begun to laugh openly. 'I wouldn't take those model planes if you paid me to haul them away. They're utterly worthless.'

'What! But Marshal Koli said . . .'

'Marshal Koli was a collector, Mr Administrator. I'm a businessman. The documents I have to sell should be worth in the neighbourhood of one hundred Ganymedian cluds. It is that or nothing.'

'Let me see it,' Mekkis said.

'One page, that's all.'

Mekkis said, 'I could have you arrested and the document taken from you by force.'

'True,' the Huckster said. 'But you would never see the other documents I could bring you; this is only one of many such lovely items.'

'Very well. My secretary will make out a cheque for you to the amount of one hundred cluds. Now let's see the thing.'

After the Huckster had gone Mekkis studied the document carefully. It appeared authentic; he recognised the writing-style of the erratic Balkani. The key, Mekkis thought; analysis of the experiments in chemotherapy which made possible his Oblivion Therapy. Great god almighty! *I'll have to see what else that young Terran has for sale*, mused the Ganymedian Administrator.

140

He did not grant an audience to Gus Swenesgard. When notified of Gus' presence he did not even bother to scan him. 'As I've already ordered,' he informed his secretary, 'give him what he wants and leave me alone.' Gus, therefore, left with a requisition for first-line autonomic and homeostatic Ganymedian attack weapons.

Mekkis did not know this, but, had he known, he would not have cared. Because a report had come in—news completely unexpected.

'Percy X and Joan Hiashi,' his wik secretary informed him, 'have escaped from Dr Balkani's establishment in Norway.' A pause and then the secretary said, 'Dr Balkani is dead.'

For a moment Mekkis ceased to think. He sat, mouth open, his tongue frozen. 'How did it happen?' he asked at last.

'Suicide, it would appear.'

'No,' Mekkis whispered. 'It can't be suicide.'

'I'm only passing on what information I got from Cultural Control,' the secretary said.

'Is there anything more?'

The secretary said, 'It seems almost certain that Percy X has returned to this bale; that has Cultural Control in a panic because it indicates that resistance to Gany rule may be much more widespread and subtle than had been previously believed. Someone managed to slip two simulcra into Balkani's establishment, one of Percy X and one of Joan Hiashi; Balkani evidently didn't recognise the switch, even though the simulcra had been built from one of his designs. There is speculation that Balkani was a double agent and that all of the wiks trained by him may be imprinted with lethal post-hypnotic suggestions. Some have already killed themselves—for no apparent reason.'

141

'Thank you,' Mekkis said in a strangled voice. He tongued off the intercom and sat for a long time in silence. All around him lay the articles, monographs, books and pamphlets of Dr Balkani, and Mekkis thought, *As long as I am alive Balkani is alive, too. What he began I will finish. The work of the man exists entire in my mind.*

Harshly, he called for his creeches. They came, scuttling and scampering and flapping, from the next room, pitifully happy to be once more noticed, once more of use to him.

'Electronics engineer,' Mekkis said.

'Yes,' squeaked the little being with the slender, delicate fingers.

'Rig up the thought amplifier that we use to contact the Great Common for short-range purposes,' he commanded. *We live always in each other's minds,* he thought, *Stuck together in a sticky mass through the Great Common, hardly existing as individuals at all.*

But I, he thought, *have become an individual; I have separated from the Great Womb and been born—as what? A true Ganymedian? A human? No; something else: a stranger in the universe, belonging nowhere. A Balkani. The Great Common turned against me, cast me out to rot away in the most unwanted corner of the system. Now,* he thought, *I can thank them for it; if I hadn't hated them I never would have seen the meaning of Dr Balkani's theories.*

Theories? No, facts. The truth, the ultimate truth of existence.

'What,' the Oracle said apprehensively, 'are you going to do with the thought amplifier when it is rigged?'

'I'm going to contact Percy X,' Mekkis informed him.

'Then,' the Oracle said with resignation, 'it is too late to turn back. The great darkness is upon us and nothing can stop it now.'

14

When the Toms perceived the angel of light descending from the heavens they fled in terror, leaving the warehouse unguarded.

'That got those superstitious rats moving,' Percy X shouted in triumph. 'Now set up a wall of fire around the warehouse to keep them out while we load up with supplies.'

'Right,' Lincoln said, moving the dials of his mechanism and concentrating.

Almost at once the flames became so hot that it was hard for the two Neeg-parts to breathe. But the fire burned without consuming. Working quickly and efficiently the two men soon had their ionocraft so heavily loaded that they knew it would be reluctant to leave the ground.

As they worked, Percy sang—one of the wordless microtonal chants that had grown out of so many cold nights in the mountains. *It's good to feel my muscles pull*, he said to himself. *Much better than to think when thought only leads to despair*. A moment later the ionocraft, with its cargo and the two men inside it, glided away from the flame-surrounded warehouse and headed, unobserved, for the mountains.

As they flew, Percy became more and more aware of the sensation of being a bird and less and less aware of being a man flying an ionocraft. He had ceased to see the craft around him or its control panel; now he even ceased to feel the steering wheel and the pedals. He forgot, for an interval, that he had ever been a man. Nothing remained but air currents, which he could see by means of tiny distortions in the background of hills and trees. He was swimming in the air, feeling its currents as stresses on some sort of transparent plastic, feeling the different levels moving against each other like the different parts in a great choral hymn.

A voice called him from somewhere far away. He recognised it as the voice of Joan Hiashi and it said, 'He knew you were listening. He's a terrible ham.' For an instant he made out her face; then that face changed, the features moving, shifting about like moist plastic under the fingers of a sculptor, and it became Joan no longer; it became Lincoln Shaw, shouting at him, 'Snap out of it! Snap out of it, Percy! We almost crashed!'

Gradually Percy returned to the ionocraft and saw the hills sweeping by on both sides of the craft. 'I thought I was a bird,' he said unsteadily.

'Yeah I know,' Lincoln said, shakily adjusting his battered horn-rimmed glasses. 'I turned off the projector just in time.'

'I was singing to Joan. And Paul Rivers, he was there, too; I flew right up to his face.'

'That's what you think, man. That wasn't Paul Rivers' face you almost bumped into. That was the face of a solid rock cliff.

'You'd better handle the controls until we get back to base camp, Percy said, perspiring; his hands had begun to shake and the motion was communicated through the sensitive controls to the ionocraft itself.

'Now you're talking,' Lincoln said, taking over.

For a time they skimmed along in silence and then Percy said, 'The food will last better, now.'

'That's one of the advantages,' Lincoln said caustically, 'of having fewer mouths to feed.'

'How many will there be when we get back?'

Lincoln said, 'Don't ask me, man.'

'All I know anymore,' Percy said, 'is that . . .' He broke off. Within his mind a voice had spoken. 'I hear a voice,' he said.

'The projector,' Lincoln said. 'Don't pay any attention to it.'

'Is that you, Percy X?' the voice asked.

'Yes,' Percy answered. There was something naggingly familiar about the voice and about the vague emotional shapes that floated behind it. For a moment he thought it was Dr Balkani and then he realised it was Mekkis, a terribly changed Mekkis—a far cry from the cool, self-assured administrator of power that Percy had faced the day of his capture. Mekkis now had strange, painful, sharp vibrations infused throughout him.

'I have a proposition for you,' Mekkis said jerkily.

'I've already heard your proposition,' Percy said, 'and I'm not buying it.'

'This,' Mekkis said, 'is different. Previously I asked you to join me; now I'd like to join you—against our mutual enemy, the Great Common of Ganymede.'

The prison of Ulvöya lay almost deserted under a grey, low, slow-moving overcast. The cell doors, even the entrances to the buildings, stood open, so that some of the bolder seagulls found themselves able to enter and roam through the long dim hallways, in search of food. The smell of their droppings had already begun to taint the chill air, and their cries echoed up and down the passageways like distant, despairing screams for help.

Hearing these cries the creeches of Marshal Koli clustered close around their master, shivering, telling themselves that no matter what happened their master would know what to do. Koli, as he lay on the analyst's couch in what formerly had been Dr Balkani's office, paid no attention to his surroundings at all, but gave himself over wholeheartedly to the not unpleasant task of cross-examining Major Ringdahl, who sat behind Balkani's desk, cold and miserable. The electric power had been turned off so they had been forced to make do with candles; the draughts that swept in under the door made the candleflames flicker and dance and constantly threaten to go out, at the same time casting demonic writhing shadows on the stone walls.

'Can you explain,' Marshal Koli demanded, nodding in the direction of the deactivated robot Percy X and what remained of the robot Joan Hiashi that lay side by side in the corner of the room, 'how those two quaint contraptions got here?'

'No,' Major Ringdahl answered. 'Unless Dr Balkani...'

'And what about the doctor's book, Major? What happened to it?'

'There's a mail robot that goes around in the morning and picks up all outgoing mail. If Balkani put the manuscript of his book in his outgoing mail basket the robot would have received it and automatically sent it off.'

'Where was the manuscript sent?'

Ringdahl said huskily, 'We have no way of determining that, sir.'

'You know where I think he sent it?' Koli arched himself into an s-curve of fury. 'I think he sent it to his co-members of a vast and previously unsuspected underground movement. I don't believe, Major Ringdahl, that you appreciate the gravity of this matter. It isn't just a question of closing down the Ulvöya operation. We can no longer rely on any of the wiks conditioned here—and that includes the better part of the human portion of the governmental structure. Without this human buffer between the rulers and the ruled our plans for this planet will be effectively stalled. If we have to do all the ruling and policing of this planet ourselves, with no human assistance, it will simply be more trouble and expense than it's worth.'

'What can you do about it?' Major Ringdahl asked.

'We can withdraw from this planet,' Koli said crisply. He signalled his carriers, and, with a sardonic nod to the major, left; his creeches trailed behind him in a straggling, scuttling procession.

Night was falling as they emerged from the building. As they made their way with difficulty to an awaiting ionocraft the Techman creech scampered up close to his master and asked, fearfully, 'Are we actually pulling out? Giving up?'

'Of course not,' Koli said. 'We will only be evacuating the planet to permit Operation Sterilisation to begin. After all our Ganymedian forces are safely out in space, I will personally supervise the systematic extinction of all life on the Earth. It will be a careful, thorough job, I assure you, and after this planet has been wiped clean, we will return to repopulate the globe with reasonable Ganymedian life forms.'

'Your wisdom is profound,' the Techman creech said, pleased.

'Predict something,' Mekkis ordered.

'There is no future.' The Oracle gave a long weary sigh.

'If you do not function,' Mekkis said, 'I can have you replaced.'

'Killed, you mean. But it doesn't matter, a few hours more or less. We are already dead, did but we know it.'

'Guard!' Mekkis called into the intercom. A moment later a human military individual entered the room. Pointing at the Oracle with a quivering tongue Mekkis said, 'Shoot him.'

'Your own death . . .' the Oracle began, but did not finish its prophecy.

'Drag the carcass out and dump it somewhere,' Mekkis instructed the guard. He felt gloomy. As soon as the guard had left he called for his electronics technician. 'Turn on the amplifier,' he instructed. 'I wish to contact Percy X.'

The electronics technician set the thought amplifier for Percy's general location and encephalic wave form, while Mekkis, aided by his dressers, slipped on the transmitting helmet.

'Percy,' he thought, concentrating deeply, his cold eyes shut.

Presently an answering thought. 'I am Percy. I am here.'

'According to all my studies,' Mekkis projected, 'the hell-weapon is our only hope of victory. I believe you ought to use it.' Carefully, he masked and scrambled any doubts he might have, projecting only his feeling of urgency.

'I'd be glad to,' Percy answered, 'if I live long enough.'

'What do you mean?'

148

'I'm under attack by your friend Gus. He's surrounded me and he's closing in with first-line Gany hardware, fully autonomic. I think this time he's finally got me.'

Mekkis concentrated and in a moment found himself looking out through Percy X's eyes. Everywhere he looked he saw robot tanks, troops and ionocrafts of all sizes and shapes. Moving in for the kill.

An army of robots and autonomic engines of war faced, on the field of battle, an army of nightmares. As the two armies tangled, Percy and Lincoln crouched in the mouth of a cave, operating an illusion projector. Scattered over the area and concealed in the cave behind him bobbed and ducked all that remained of Percy's Neegparts. So many had defected . . . and now, peering down into the valley below, Percy saw that others had their hands up, had begun to go over to the enemy.

'You, too?' Percy demanded, grabbing Lincoln by the arm. 'You turning against me, too?'

'Keerist, I'm sitting here working this damn nightmare box and you ask me if I've turned against you!'

'If you do,' Percy said in a low, threatening voice, 'I'll kill you.'

'You'll never kill me, man,' Lincoln said. 'I'm the only one around who has the guts to tell you the truth about yourself.'

'I don't know what got into me.' Percy shook his head, trying to clear his mind. *My head doesn't seem quite right*, he realised. *They must be using some new kind of nerve gas on us.* He saw, then, that Lincoln was looking at him with real concern. 'I can see it in your mind,' Percy said. 'You think I'm getting paranoid.'

Lincoln glanced away, saying nothing.

'Look out there,' Percy grated, gesturing at the valley

149

where now the muffled thunder of high-velocity explosives could be heard. 'Is it a delusion that everyone's against me? Am I just imagining all those tanks and ionocrafts? Am I just imagining all those Neeg-parts going over to the other side? It's me against the universe! One man! And it's no delusion.'

'Okay, Percy,' Lincoln said, with a mixture in his voice of admiration and revulsion. 'You win. I guess that as you say . . .'

'Wait!' Percy cut in; his battle-trained eye had turned once again to the valley below. 'Look—those idiots those idiots down there aren't using the illusion projectors; they don't have a chance without them!'

Even as the two men watched, the leading column of autonomic tanks burst through Percy's lines and came rumbling toward them. 'Look out,' Lincoln shouted. They're drawing a bead on us!'

Not one second too soon the two Neeg-parts leaped back into the cave, while, behind them, the cave entrance exploded in an inferno of heat and dust and flying fragments.

'We've had it!' shouted someone in the swirling clouds of dust.

Another voice followed it. 'Surrender!'

Other voices joined in. 'Surrender! Surrender! We haven't got a chance!'

Then Percy X's voice cut through the confusion. 'Fight, you yellow-bellies! Fight to the last man!' But from the sound of scrambling feet it was clear that few —if any—intended to follow his commands. 'Come on,' he said to Lincoln. 'We'll go farther back into the cave and wait for them there; they can't bring their damn tanks and ionocrafts in here—its narrow and its complicated and I know every inch of it.'

'You're the boss,' Lincoln said grimly. They set off into the depths of the mountain, making repeated spot-checks with their portable arc light. Finally Percy said, 'Okay, let's dig in here.'

They crouched together behind a smooth stalagmite and held laser rifles in readiness. Percy muttered under his breath, 'I sure wish I had that hell-weapon here.'

'I'm glad you don't,' Lincoln said. 'It's encouraging to know that even if we're going to die somebody will be left.'

'Even if it's just worms and wiks and traitors?' Percy asked.

Lincoln said, 'Even if it's just worms and wiks and traitors.' His voice sounded tired.

They had no opportunity to continue their conversation, because at that moment, in the darkness of the cave, they heard the unmistakable hum of electric motors and the tramp of heavy metal feet. 'Here they come,' Percy said; he and Lincoln raised their laser rifles to their shoulders.

Percy fired first, aiming where he knew the entrance to their chamber lay. The robot exploded beautifully; by the flames that leaped up from it they could make out the other robots sneaking forward behind it. There seemed to be no end of them. Again and again the two men fired, but still the metal giants advanced, unceremoniously crushing underfoot the wreckage of their disabled comrades. The air filled with bitter, acrid smoke and the smell of burning and shorted wiring; Percy and Lincoln could hardly breathe: they coughed and coughed helplessly while the tears poured from their eyes and traced lines in the dust which coated their cheeks. The heat of the burning machines was rapidly making it unbearably hot in this narrow, enclosing space; however, the two of them, drenched with sweat, continued firing.

It was Percy who first ran out of charge; he pulled the trigger and swore at the top of his voice when nothing happened. Roughly he grabbed Lincoln's rifle, only to find that it, too, had only two more good blasts left. 'Have you got anything else?' Percy demanded.

'Nothing that'll stop those things,' Lincoln answered.

Helpless now, they watched the metal juggernauts lurched triumphantly towards them.

15

Late in the afternoon the ionocraft bearing Paul Rivers and Joan Hiashi swept down out of the cloudless sky and settled onto the street in front of Gus Swenesgard's seedy, run-down hotel. Paul pushed open the door and climbed out, then turned to Joan and said, 'Stay out of sight. I don't want Gus to see you.'

'Okay,' she said dreamily, lying down like a child on the seat. 'I don't care for that musty old place anyhow. I think I'll stay out here in the sunshine.'

'Fine,' Paul said as he started for the sagging front porch of the hotel with its familiar flight of broken steps. *Judging from the smoke up in the mountains,* he reflected, *the Neeg-parts are fairly hard-pressed. If Percy is captured alive again they'll just skin him and be done with it.* Nervously he fingered the laser pistol in his pocket. *If Percy is brought this far alive,* he realised, *there'll be no choice for me. I'll have to burn him out of existence.*

Sighing, he climbed the rickety steps and crossed the porch. *I think,* he said to himself, *I'll stick close to Gus; if Percy is captured, sooner or later he'll turn up here now that Gus, it seems, is the actual functioning top man in this bale.*

As he entered the lobby Gus called out to him, 'Hey, welcome back, sir. It's not every day someone comes back to this hotel for a second time.' He chuckled, evidently in an unusually good mood.

'It's so quiet here,' Paul said carefully. 'So restful.'

'Not today it ain't,' chortled Gus with a coarse wink. 'Here.' He handed Paul a cigar, not his usual cheap make but an authentic hand-rolled Cuesta Rey. 'Help me celebrate.'

Paul accepted the cigar but did not light it. 'Celebrate what?'

'The death of Percy X,' announced the portly, flushed little balding man. 'And the s-s-surrender of the Neeg-parts.' In his excitement he stammered over his words, trying to get them out all at once. 'What all the Gany occupation forces put together couldn't do, ol' Gus Swenesgard did without hardly raising a sweat.' He noticed the unlit cigar and added, 'Say, if you don't smoke, maybe you'll have a drink.'

'I'm in,' Paul said. *I wonder,* he thought, *if he really has succeeded in wiping out the Neeg-parts and Percy —and if so, where he has the body.* Gus now handed him a glass of straight Scotch, grinning broadly; Paul tasted it, then set it down. *I'll need,* he thought grimly, *all my wits about me in coping with this wily old crook.* 'How do you know,' he said aloud, 'that Percy X is dead?'

'Well,' admitted Gus candidly, 'I ain't actually seen the corpse, but the autonomic control central radioed me an hour or more ago and told me all effective resistance had ceased up there. Percy ain't among the prisoners, so he must be dead.'

'Couldn't he have escaped?'

Gus shook his head so vigorously that his jowls danced. 'N-n-not on your l-l-life. They had him trapped in a cave—no way out. And I sent in robots to track him down if alive or sort him out from the other bodies if dead. I expect I'll get the report any minute now. Meanwhile I think I'll stroll over and tell that worm, Mekkis, the good news. Want to come along?'

'No thanks,' Paul said; he did not care to get within range of a telepathic Gany.

'Suit yourself,' Gus said, and stumped out.

Aboard the most modern ionocraft taxi in the bale Gus rode over to military headquarters. As the taxi descended, he could not help noticing that the usually busy complex of installations appeared oddly deserted. Nothing stirred. *Strange*, he thought, as he landed.

At the first opportunity he took a human wik to one side and asked, 'Hey, what's going on here? Where is everybody?'

'Don't you know?' the wik, a manual labourer, said, amazed at such ignorance. 'The Ganys are pulling out.'

'What? Leaving the bale?' Gus was dumbfounded.

'Hell no. Leaving this planet.'

Before Gus could recover enough to ask further questions the workman had departed to resume his work, that of crating up what appeared to be microfilm documents of an official nature. Despite his shock Gus could not help noticing, with a calculating, practical eye, that the Ganys were apparently leaving a good deal of valuable items behind: not only vehicles and the housing installations but even weapons—of advanced Gany design. *I think*, he reflected, *I'll ask my old friend Mekkis if I can maybe take all this junk off his hands . . . so to speak. I know how a feller hates to have a lot of useless odds and ends littered around everywhere when he's trying to move.*

For the first time in weeks Gus found himself admitted to Mekkis' private chamber. The Administrator, coiled peacefully, appeared to be reading a Terran book but looked up with a cordial smile as Gus entered.

'I understand you're moving,' Gus blurted out.

'Do you? But I'm not. Not at all.' The Administrator's tone held haughty aloofness; the subject obviously touched some deep, cold wellspring in him.

'But the workman told me . . .'

'The entire Ganymedian occupation force with the exception of me is withdrawing. Since I have not merged with the Great Common for quite some time I have no notion why. Nor do I really care. In any case, let me assure you that I, and my necessary entourage of personal creeches, are staying.'

Gus said, 'I don't understand. Don't all you Ganys act as a . . .'

'I have scientific reasons for detaching myself. An experiment begun by the late, great Doctor Rudolph Balkani remains to be completed. Can I swear you to secrecy?'

'What? Oh yeah; sure.' Gus nodded.

With his jaws, Mekkis lifted up a thick typescript manuscript; he deposited it, with effort, before him on his desk. 'I obtained this from Balkani's New York publisher. It arrived today, arranged for by persons working in my behalf. This is the sole copy . . . of Doctor Balkani's final statement, his *Oblivion Therapy*—entirely mine, now. I see in your mind that this does not mean anything to you or even interest you; what you care about is power. You want this office, don't you?'

'Um,' Gus said sheepishly, gesturing.

'Be my guest, Mr Swenesgard. I am vacating these buildings shortly, just on the off-chance that some of my so-called "fellow" Ganymedians might come looking for me.' With the faint hint of a sneer he concluded, 'This place, Mr Swenesgard, is all yours.'

'Here he comes,' Paul Rivers said to Joan Hiashi; she ducked down in the front seat of their ionocraft once more as Paul got swiftly out. In the slanting rays of the setting sun Gus came shuffling along, obviously somewhat drunk. Paul walked towards him thinking, *I suppose he's starting to celebrate his victory already.*

A few people moved here and there, mostly dutiful Toms who made it a point to mind their own business; nobody appeared to notice—or care—that the kingfish of the bale manifested himself in this condition. It had probably happened before.

'Hi, Gus,' Paul said.

Gus halted, swaying unsteadily and blinking at Paul without comprehension. 'Who're you?' Gus demanded.

'We talked briefly several hours ago,' Paul said. 'And for several days I stayed at your hotel.' He made his tone firm, so that it would penetrate. 'I'm Doctor Paul Rivers.'

'Oh yeah, I remember now.' Gus nodded. 'And I, Doctor, am the future emperor of the world.'

What, Paul asked himself acutely, *does he mean by that?*

Gus placed a beefy hand on Paul's shoulder and,

waving his finger under Paul's nose, said, 'They're leaving.'

'Who's leaving?' He had to brace himself against the weight of Gus' heavy hand.

'The worms. And when they go, you know who's going to take over around here? Me; that's who: *me.*' Gus released his grip on Paul's shoulder and staggered back a step. 'The day of the Thing on Horseback has passed.' His slurred speech had suddenly sharpened into distinct clarity. But only momentarily.

Is he drunk, Paul wondered, *or is he telling the truth?* 'Come on, Gus,' he said, placing Gus' arm over his shoulder. 'I'll help you into the hotel.'

When, with a grunt of relief, Paul deposited the bulky and stumbling Gus onto a couch in the hotel lobby the clerk at the desk, like everyone else in town, pretended to see nothing.

'I'm the one,' Gus began again, half to Paul and half to himself. 'The one with all the autonomic weapons the Ganys gave me to fight Percy X. And I'm the one, now, who has all those crazy mental weapons Percy had, too. I'm the man'—and here he paused to burp—'with the power.' Again, all at once, his voice cleared into focus; his eyes ceased to show their usual glaze. 'I'm going to go on TV, prime time. When the Ganys pull out the people won't know what to do; they'll be looking for a leader, somebody to take the place of the worms. They'll be thirsting for solid American-human leadership from someone they know and trust, someone who knows them and is one of them.'

After an interval Paul said, 'That's not a bad pitch.'

'I know,' Gus said.

The Man on Horseback, Paul thought, *replacing the Thing on Horseback; Gus is right—this is the time for*

157

him to appear. Gus would be the familiar replacing the alien. Humanity incarnate, with all its limitations and faults, but indubitably real.

'I can see it now,' Gus said thickly, his eyes once more filmed over, his head wagging unsteadily. 'The TV show begins; I put in my appearance while the announcer reads a little something I scratched out ahead of time—informing them as to my victory over the Neeg-parts, a victory even the Ganys couldn't achieve.' He belched once again and had to cease talking; his face red and large, seemed to swell to even greater proportions. 'Hey, you leaving, Doc?' He blinked.

It isn't every day, Paul thought, *that I get to talk to the future emperor of Earth. But if I don't get out of here and do something, and fast, there may not be any Earth left to rule over.*

Ten minutes later Paul Rivers, with Joan beside him, skimmed over starlit fields towards the mountains. He placed the ionocraft on full automatic pilot and got out Ed Newkom's thought amplifier.

'Why are you doing that?' Joan asked, with mild curiosity.

Paul said, 'I have a nagging fear, which I can't get rid of, that Percy X is still alive.'

'If he wants to use his hell-weapon,' Joan said, 'let him. What difference does it make, really?'

Can it be true, Paul asked himself, *that the possible extinction of most of the human race is a matter of complete indifference to her? Maybe that's what she wants: final complete oblivion for everyone.*

'You need to save the world,' she said remotely. She glanced then at him, as if he were a retarded child.

Ignoring the look—he could not answer it—he set to

158

work with the amplifier, trying to tune in on Percy X.

'Hello, Paul,' came Percy's thought, almost immediately.

'Percy, I want . . .' he began, but Percy X cut him off.

'I know. You want me to hold off on the hell-weapon.'

'That's right.'

Percy X's thoughts came through heavy with weariness. 'I almost wish I could. But I can't; it's our last chance to defeat the worms. My little so-called "army" got wiped out and they damn near finished off me. I simply have nothing left to fight with but the hell-weapon, and I'm not going to give up, man; I'm not going to give up!'

'But,' Paul transmitted, 'the worms are leaving.'

'For how long?' demanded Percy X bitterly. 'They'll be back. And meanwhile we'll know they're up there, ready to return and take over whenever they feel like it.'

'You can't prevent that even if you use the hell-weapon; it'll only get the Ganys here on Earth. The others who are still on Ganymede won't be harmed, and, like you say, they can launch a new attack against Earth any time they want to.'

A wave of glee rushed from Percy's mind to his own. 'That's not so. Before I turn on the machine my good buddy Mekkis is going to key his own mind into the group mind of the Ganymedian Great Common. Anything that happens to the mind of Mekkis, here on Earth, will happen to the entire Ganymedian ruling class at the same time—and the ruling class does all the thinking on Ganymede. Without them the creeches will be lucky if they can avoid slipping back to the level of the Stone Age; what can a body do when you cut off its head, Doctor?'

159

'But the human race,' Paul said. 'You'll destroy it, too.'

'Those Ganys are totally dependent on their creeches; they're weak. Men, who are more or less used to taking care of themselves, will eventually manage to pull out of it—but the Ganys won't.' Percy paused, and Paul felt a wave of wistful accidental flow from Percy to himself. 'I hope, Doc, that you're one of the strong ones. If so, I'll be seeing you.'

'Yes,' Paul said, 'you'll be seeing me.' But nothing remained of Percy X's thought pattern except the meaningless blur of an expert scramble pattern.

Marshal Koli drifted slowly through the control cabin of the flagship of the Ganymedian space fleet, the helmet on his head connecting him, through the ship's encephalic amplifier, to the Great Common of the home world and to all other members of the ruling élite, wherever they might be.

An entire block of minds, the leaders of the clock faction, spoke in Koli's mind as a single voice. 'Is the evacuation complete?'

'With one exception,' Koli answered. 'Mekkis.'

'Mekkis? Mekkis?' The Great Common searched itself and found one missing mind. One and only one. Nobody wished to be left out of this vital operation; even the sick, who were sometimes excused, were here, adding their touch of yellow suffering to the rainbow of blended spirit. 'What happened to him?' the polyencephalic entity inquired.

'Went native,' Koli informed them—or rather it. 'I for one will not miss him.'

'Nor will we,' came the massed voice of the Council.

'I will miss him,' said Major Cardinal Zency, dissenting.

The Electors at the bench bathed him in a wave of soothing condolence, to which he reacted, to their surprise, with resentment.

'Is the missile in readiness?' came the massed thought of the clock faction leaders again.

'I am checking it over now,' Marshal Koli answered; he drifted over the gleaming cylinder of destruction which now reposed before the airlock, ready to be moved forward into launching position. 'Look through my eyes, fellow Ganymedians, and see for yourself.' Koli could feel a multitude of beings behind his eyes, watching everything he watched, feeling everything he felt. They would even taste what he tasted when his tongue touched the firing button that would launch the missile into space.

The flagship shifted slightly in space, its motion sending the crew, including Koli, drifting slowly towards one side of it. Marshal Koli, well accustomed to such things, paid no attention; his mind was busy reviewing once again, with good measure of satisfaction, the chain of events which would follow his touching the firing button. The missile, once launched, would move quickly to a point near the Earth but outside Earth's atmosphere; there it would stabilise itself in an orbit that would keep it fixed directly between Earth and the Sun. Then, automatically, it would project an electromagnetic field in the aural spectrum which would cause the rays of the Sun to bend, to warp out of their normal path, so that not a single ray of sunlight would reach the Earth. *The seas will freeze*, Koli thought, *right down to the bottom—and not only the seas but the atmosphere, the very air the Terrans breathe. The atmosphere will drift down like a pale snow until Earth is as bare of breathable gas as the planet Pluto.*

Then, and only then, would the aural field within the missile be turned off and the rays of the Sun allowed once again to reach the surface of Earth. The atmosphere would melt, become first a liquid and then, once again, a gas. The seas would melt, the planet would slowly, over a period of almost a century, become habitable again; Ganymedians would return and colonise it, this time solely with imported life forms from the home world. It had certainly been a major mistake, reflected the Great Common, to allow the native life forms to live, in the vain hope they might become useful creeches. The mistake, if they ever found other habitable worlds, would not be repeated.

From now on the policy would be: *Turn off the Sun. And wait.*

Koli had saved one item from Earth, a perfect souvenir of the human race that would now, with the extinction of that race, become very soon a rarity of incredible value. A complete collection of the early short comedies of the original Three Stooges, pre-World War Three. He licked his chops in anticipation of the envy on his friends' faces when he projected these films, over and over again, in his private villa back home. *What do I care*, he thought smugly, *if they become a little bored? I'll say to them, 'This is what mankind was like,' and I'll have them; yes, I'll have them. They won't be able to argue with the authentic films which the Terrans themselves made. And they'll be forced to say, whether they like it or not, 'Koli, when you exterminated the Earth creatures, you did the right thing.'*

I don't want to kill you, Paul Rivers thought, his palms

162

sweating against the cool metal of the laser rifle. *But I will if I have to.*

'I see,' Percy X said. He half-sat, half-fell against a rough, pitted rock-surface and watched the spinning world come slowly to rest.

'I've been following you,' Paul said. 'I spotted you from the air. You must be tired; you didn't even detect us telepathically.'

'Yeah, I am tired,' Percy panted. But Paul could see that he had begun to regain possession of himself, sizing up the situation like a brilliant, trapped, cat-like animal. First the Neeg-part leader studied Paul—and his laser rifle—and then the parked ionocraft behind Paul and at last Joan Hiashi, who, at that moment, had knelt down to inspect something on the loose, rocky soil of the hillside. 'Hello, Joan,' Percy said, but she did not even look at him, let alone answer.

'She's found an anthill,' Paul Rivers said. 'She's taken quite an interest in ants lately.'

'They're upset,' Joan said tonelessly. 'They can sense something coming.'

'I see in your mind,' Percy said to Paul Rivers, 'that you haven't destroyed the hell-weapon, which is what you came here to do.'

'We only got here a few minutes before you did,' Paul pointed out. 'Yes, I know it's in a cave over there.' He gestured with his free hand. 'I've got a metal-tropic detection apparatus in my ship. You're not going to get to use it, even if I have to fry you with this laser rifle.'

Percy had begun to breathe evenly now, and his eyes, which had been dull and feverish a moment before, had become alert and penetrating. 'Tell me, Paul,' he said slowly, calculatingly. 'Have you ever tried to shoot a telepath before?'

163

'Get into the ionocraft,' Paul ordered, raising the gun a hair.

Ignoring the command Percy continued, 'It isn't easy to shoot someone who can read your mind, Doctor. I can tell, an instant before you pull the trigger, where you plan to aim that gun—before you aim it.' He smiled and added, 'And if you're really going to shoot.'

'Get into the ionocraft,' Paul Rivers repeated, but he thought, *Suppose he's right; suppose I can't shoot him.*

'I don't think you can,' Percy X said. 'Put the gun down, Paul, I don't want to hurt you any more than you want to hurt me.'

Paul had been aware of a feeling of unreality for some time now, but had put it down as an after-effect of some nearby, recent usage of an illusion projector in this mountain region. *However, in that case,* he realised, *the effect should be wearing off, instead of steadily increasing, as it seems to be.*

'I notice the same thing,' Percy X said. 'It's as if something is wrong with time, like there's no clear separation between past and future.' He had a puzzled expression on his face; his eyes worked, darting and penetrating, as he considered the matter. Then all at once he started visibly. 'You know what it means, don't you, Paul?'

'No,' Paul said guardedly, never once taking his eyes off the crouching Neeg-part leader.

'I've already won,' Percy X said. 'Somewhere up ahead of us in time I've already turned on the machine, and as we get closer to it we begin to feel its emanations. Didn't Balkani say that space and time are just illusions produced by selective attention? This proves it, don't you see? And it proves there's no way to stop me. *My turning on the machine is inevitable.*'

There is only one thing I can do, Paul Rivers realised

164

with dismay. *If I'm going to keep him from killing us all I've got to shoot him. But I can't, not unarmed and helpless as he is.*

'Helpless?' Percy X said sardonically. He started to his feet.

Paul pulled the trigger, but when the searing blast bored a hole through the rock behind Percy X the man was not there; an instant before he had sprung out of danger, rolling over once and leaping to his feet, just a little closer to Paul.

'You see?' Percy X said, taking another step forward.

There was something wrong with the light. Instead of coming straight down it seemed bent, as if forming a cone of force between Percy X and himself. And at the same time Paul felt a curious numbness descending over his mind; he had to fight to keep his attention on what he intended to do.

Percy X took another careful step forward. 'Go ahead, Paul buddy. Shoot me if you can.'

Paul fired again. This time Percy jumped slightly to one side, graceful and lithe.

'Hey, Paul buddy,' Percy gasped, 'you know something? Mekkis is tuned in on me now, watching you through my eyes, ready to link up with the Ganymedian group mind just before I turn on the machine. We're really going to zap them, man; we're really going to give it to them. He tells me that space looks funny where he is, too, and time seems to be getting mixed up. He says that he had an Oracle who said this would happen, so it's going to happen, Paul baby, and you better believe it.'

Percy X took another step forward. He stood, now, perhaps nine feet away. *One good leap*, Paul realised, *and he's got me.*

'You are so right, man,' Percy said, and tensed for the leap.

Paul fired, just burning Percy's shirt, then fired again, missing him completely. He had no opportunity to fire a third time; Percy X felled him with a judo chop that sent him sprawling in the dust, virtually unconscious. The last thing Paul saw before he blacked out was Joan Hiashi frowning at him and saying, 'Watch out; you almost fell on the anthill.'

They're so careless, Joan Hiashi thought. She watched without saying anything further as Percy X snatched up Paul's laser rifle and threw it over a nearby slope; the big Neeg-part leader was laughing now, with the gloating snarl of a victor, and he continued laughing, but more quietly, to himself, as he strode towards the entrance of the cave.

Joan returned her attention to the ant colony on the ground before her. And frowned.

Something had further upset the ants. They had begun to wander aimlessly, instead of going about their business in their usual orderly fashion.

She heard a moan and glanced questioningly up again.

Paul Rivers had dragged himself to his feet, shaking his head vigorously in an effort to clear it. He peered into the cave, saw Percy X at the entrance and, although still by no means recovered from the judo chop, started towards Percy X at a clumsy, weaving run. Percy X looked back, saw Paul coming, and sprang through the entrance into the dark interior of the cavern. A moment later Paul, too, had disappeared into the cave; Joan heard the sound of scuffling and then a strangled, half-human cry, followed by silence.

166

Hearing nothing more after an interval she bent down to examine the ants more closely. Suddenly a bird fell nearby, still fluttering; then another and another.

With a trace of amusement Joan thought, *It's raining birds.*

A thought came to Marshal Koli from one of the leaders of the clock faction, a thought tinged with annoyance. 'Mekkis just tuned in.'

Koli shrugged. *What difference,* he thought, *does that make?*

He stretched out his tongue towards the firing button, noticing with no real alarm a peculiar effect of light and a sensation of *déjà vu,* as if he had done this same thing many times before.

It's just the excitement, he decided.

Then, it seemed to him, the button started to move away from him. His tongue grew longer and longer, reaching for it, but still it moved away. Now his tongue had become longer than his body and was yet growing; the button, however, remained no closer than before. With a madness born out of panic Koli guessed—correctly—that the button was moving away from him not in space but in time.

What's going on here? he demanded of the Great Common, and, as if to answer his question, he suddenly found himself in the mind of the turncoat Mekkis.

Mekkis thought, *All right, you great and glorious Common. I, Rudolph Balkani, am killing you, and you know that I am killing you and you will go on knowing it for a long time. Into the sensory withdrawal tank, all of you worms!*

Trying to remember who he himself was, Koli found that his name had escaped him. He knew only that it was neither Mekkis nor Balkani; he was someone who had intended to push a button. *Ah, I know,* he thought; *I am Percy X! And he found himself reaching with a* dark-skinned finger for a push-button on a small but somehow infinitely potent machine in a cave within Terran mountains.

And then the light bent and bent and bent, making a tube of greenish grey, a tunnel down which the one huge dark-skinned finger slowly moved, year after year.

If you decide to use the thing, he thought, *don't tell me. I don't want to know.*

Then he felt the needle enter his Percy-Koli-Balkani arm.

The dark finger at last reached the button, while a cloud of eyes watched in mute horror and all the stars in space screamed in pain-ecstasy. The dark finger pushed the button, while armies of pyrotechnic phantasms flickered in and out of being like a movie rushing through a projector at breakneck speed: whole scenes appeared superimposed over one another. And music sounded, too, also playing itself out at a frantic pace, so high-pitched that only an animal should have been able to hear it . . . yet he could hear it anyhow.

And then the finger broke, and the bent light, unable to take any more stress, broke also, and as the sound abuptly faded out and the light dimmed away to nothingness his last thought sounded in the emptiness. *Who am I?*

Becoming darkness, he could not answer his own question, because darkness does not speak. Nor think. Nor feel. It only sees.

16

Gus Swenesgard stood before the cracked bureau mirror in his room, the finest in the hotel, and toasted himself in expensive pre-war Cutty Sark Scotch. *To the future world ruler*, he said to himself, and drained the tall cracked glass. An unnatural lighting effect began to manifest itself, a sort of tunnel vision combined with a greying of the light; Gus, however, ignored it, supposing it to be only a consequence of the liquor.

This stuff, he reflected with slurred approval, *has really got the old puzoom!*

Then the lights winked out.

I'd better call one of the maintenance Toms, he thought with annoyance.

But when he tried to speak, nothing happened. It was as if, he realised, he had no vocal cords, or even any tongue or lips. He tried to move his hand up to touch his face—only to find that his hand, also, was missing.

And, he discovered, so were his feet and legs and body.

He listened, and heard not the slightest sound in the darkness. Not even the beating of his own heart. *Good God*, he thought. *I'm dead!*

He strained to make out something, anything, even if it consisted of nothing more than a figment of his own mind. The only item, however, which he could conjure up appeared to be a faint after-image of that which he had been watching at the moment the darkness came: his own reflection in the cracked old hotel mirror.

Now, experiencing himself as—not a person—but a disembodied ghost, he stared at his pseudo-reflection and felt sudden and enormous aversion. All that flesh, that sweating ugly, bloated flesh! He sprang back from it, watched with relief as it grew smaller and dimmer in the distance.

A detached feeling of freedom came over him, as if he could now, having shed his solid body, fly through space and even time without hindrance.

So this is what it's like, he said to himself, *to be an angel.*

There has been a terrible mistake, Mekkis thought in the blackness.

This in no way resembled what he had anticipated on the basis of Dr Balkani's *Oblivion Therapy*. He had expected horrors, hallucinations, a variety of grotesque and fantastic images or perhaps light phenomena composed of whirling discs of pure colour. All that he had read in the papers, books and monographs of Balkani, plus all that he had heard about the illusion projectors used by the Neeg-parts . . .

But nothing, Mekkis thought. *'Nothing' is not right.*

Even more painful than the experience itself was the thought that Balkani had been wrong, fundamentally wrong.

What deluded game have I been playing with myself? he wondered. *I'm not Balkani. I'm not even a worm called Mekkis. I am a part, not a whole; I am just one of many organs in the great body called the Common, but I am a cancerous organ, and now I've succeeded in killing the entity of which I am a part.*

Without the aid of creeches no Ganymedian of the ruling class could survive more than a few days. And in this darkness neither he nor anyone else could summon a single creech.

This is death, Mekkis thought: *death for all of us. But it's not as I imagined it would be. I thought I would be able to savour the agonies of my enemies in the Common; I believed it would be a grand and spectacular doom, like the final chords of something made of music. But it is not.*

It is nothing, absolutely nothing. And I am utterly alone in it.

Somewhere in the desolation of the Ganymedian Administrator's mind a voice seemed to be saying, 'Your death . . . will be much worse.' The Oracle. And it spoke the truth.

I've failed, Paul Rivers thought, lying buried in the darkness. *I had a grip on his throat but he was too strong for me and we were too close to the machine. Somehow he managed to reach it and turn it on. And now he's stopped the clock at last.*

However, Paul did not panic; he did not give up quite yet. He relaxed his mind and tried to think as clearly as possible. And, because of the absolute lack of interference and distraction, this proved easy to do.

It would seem, he decided, *that my autonomic nervous system is maintaining my body satisfactorily, since my mind is still functioning too well to be under the influence of any difficulty emanating from my somatic body. In that case, my body, like my mind, is also perfectly functional—though I have no way of knowing if it can obey the commands of my brain.*

Experimentally, he ordered his hand to move in the direction of the machine, as he remembered it, but instantly ran into a cancelling factor; he did not know any longer which way was up and which was down, let alone in which direction he would find the machine.

Without sensory feedback he could not act.

And yet, he thought, *if I thrash at random, the odds are good that I might accidentally come in contact with the machine, hit it and possibly break it. It's a reasonably delicate construct, as I recall from my brief glimpse of it.*

For a considerable time Paul Rivers sent out signals to his body, commanding that it gyrate, then to kick, then flail its arms. Nothing, as far as he could determine, happened; he could not even sense ground under his feet—gravity, that fundamental ubiquity, seemed to have become suspended.

He noticed, then, a slight feeling of dizziness.

It might be an indication of exertion, he thought with a flash of hope—and redoubled his efforts. Still nothing happened.

The longer that device stays on, he realised, *the more damage it will do; the effect must be radiating concentrically and God knows where it will weaken and hence terminate. I've got to think of something.*

A stray thought drifted into his mind. According to Balkani's theories, Joan Hiashi, because she had been detached from the shared reality by Oblivion Therapy, must be immune to the impulse of the machine. *That* means, he realised, *that Joan could turn it off.*

He instructed his voice to shout and his lips to form words. 'Joan! Turn off the machine!' Again and again he sent out the orders to his body, having no idea whether or not he was actually inducing a palpable sound. He kept it up for what subjectively seemed at least an hour ... but still the blackness continued.

Again he paused to think. The key, if one existed, lay in Balkani's theories somewhere. But where? *I wish*, he said to himself, *I had studied Oblivion Therapy and*

Centerpoint Theory more intensively, instead of merely skimming them as I did.

Centerpoint Theory.

That might be it.

According to Balkani's Centerpoint hypothesis, a short-cut existed through which contact would be possible between any particle of matter and any other particle, no matter how distant. It was through this Centerpoint that the aural vibrations passed in long range telepathy. Hence, on the basis of this theory, Balkani had managed to train quite a number of people—such as Percy X—to penetrate minds at a considerable distance. But actually the theory implied that anyone, under the proper conditions, might be capable of creating telepathic contact. After all, everyone held a relationship to the Centerpoint.

That means, Paul realised, *that I might function as a telepath, at least theoretically. Assuming Balkani was correct.*

Again his thoughts turned to Joan Hiashi. He could not be, of course, certain that she had remained unaffected by the machine, but if she was unaffected, that meant that, at this moment, she might be the sole person in the system worth contacting. To contact anyone else would simply be to share his blindness, to merge it with theirs.

How had Balkani claimed that individuality was established? By selective awareness. *I am Paul Rivers,* he realised, *because I am unaware of the sensations being experienced by someone else, say by Joan Hiashi. Ordinarily my own direct sensations would drown out anything I might pick up from her. But now, when I have no sensations, even faint impressions that she may be undergoing will be infinitely stronger than my own.*

173

He began by imagining himself to be a woman.

I am small, delicate, vulnerable, he told himself. *I perceive reality in the yin mode, rather than the yang. I am sensitive, flowing, graceful.*

It was not hard, he discovered, to hallucinate all these sensations with perfect conviction, since no real sensory impressions existed to counter them.

And now, he decided, *that I am a woman, I must individualise, become a specific woman. And I know which major character trait it is that delineates Joan. It is detachment. She is the most detached woman on the planet. So I, to become her, must also be detached . . . but I must not become so detached that I, like her, am indifferent to the fate of mankind.*

How easily my personality splits, he discovered. He had always thought that only a schizophrenic could achieve it, but actually it appeared to be the most simple act in the world—at least in this world that surrounded him now.

On the other hand, he thought with grim amusement, *perhaps I am a schizophrenic and just never knew it.*

Then, abruptly, he felt something. A very faint, yet somehow vital sensation; he could tell instantly that its source did not lie in his own imagination. Cold. And pressure. He was seated on something. Something hard. The sensations came too intense to be forced mental constructs; he *was* a woman. And, opening his eyes, he knew that the woman was Joan.

There, in the dirt before him, wandered ants, completely disorganised, some on their backs kicking their feet helplessly in the air, some scrambling blindly, aimlessly about. The sky had darkened considerably, which meant that some time, probably hours, had already passed. Joan sat listening to the ebb and fall of a great throng of animal screams and moans and wails that echoed and re-echoed from the surrounding woods, and Paul, through her ears, heard their travail, too. He felt her pleasure at the sound, her enjoyment of it as music, her indifference to the suffering that it represented. In his revulsion to this obliqueness he almost drew back from contact with her, almost broke the delicate link between their two minds.

It is not my job, he realised, *to judge her.* And with this understanding he found himself once again fully aware of all that she sensed. And thought. That, to him, constituted the strangest part; her thoughts could have been those of a creature which had evolved on another world entirely: they seemed so alien. Yet there was something familiar about them.

There's been a part of me like that, he reflected. *A part of me that only wants to watch, never to act.*

All right, Joan, he thought. *Watch this.* He sent a mental command to the girl's right hand, telling it to rise. It fluttered a little but remained where it was.

Let it happen, Joan, he thought strongly, with all his will in fact.

She let it happen; slowly her hand rose to hang before her face, while she gazed at it in wonder and delight, thinking that it had moved all by itself. No resistance existed in her; whatever he willed her body to do, that it did, while she simply enjoyed the sensation of being possessed by a spirit which was not herself.

He told her body to get up. It got up. He told her body to walk towards the cave; it walked towards the cave.

How strange it feels, Paul thought, *to experience reality through another person's body and percept-system. I need to make constant allowances for her smaller size and lighter weight, as well as for the special femi-*

175

nine swing that comes from her differently jointed pelvis.
He now entered the cave—and stopped, trying to penetrate the deep blackness ahead. As his pupils dilated he saw something that shocked him more than anything else he had seen during these last days. He saw himself.

The body of Paul Rivers lay next to the body of Percy X. But the body of Paul Rivers breathed. The body of Percy X did not.

Can that be me? Paul asked himself. Both bodies were covered with still-wet blood, and Paul, after the first shock, was able to piece together what had happened. When the machine had gone on, Paul had been hanging onto Percy X; when Paul began thrashing, trying to break the machine, he had instead beaten and kicked Percy viciously—had in fact brought about his death. Without either of the two men being aware of what was happening.

His own body had not escaped unharmed; Paul, making use of Joan's body, bent over to take a close look. Every finger had been broken and the arms were a mass of cuts and abrasions where Paul had smashed them futilely against the rough-stone floor of the cave.

Carefully making his way forward he reached out and switched off the machine.

And exploded in pain!

The instant the machine sank into silence he found himself once again in his own damaged body, his mind bombarded by pain-signals from a thousand sources at once.

Mercifully, he fainted after only a few moments.

'They're dead,' the medical creech said with a sigh. 'Every single member of the limbless élite is dead.' He gazed out of the porthole at the other ships of the line that drifted aimlessly in space nearby. In the distance hung the planet Earth, still green; still, seemingly, a plum ripe for the picking, if anyone happened to wish to conquer a planet.

'But why?' timidly asked one of the navigator creeches.

The medical creech shrugged. 'Something came through the Great Common. When it reached Marshal Koli I was currently in telepathic contact with him; I saw it, the great darkness without end. Of course I broke contact immediately; it would have destroyed me as well.'

'Why did not Marshal Koli break contact?' a second navigator creech inquired. 'He also might have saved hmself that way.'

The medical creech propelled itself away from the porthole. 'The ruling élite does not do that; in times of danger it merges into the polyencephalic mode. In this case, the more frightened they became the more they tried to lose themselves in unity—and thereby exposing themselves to whatever malignant force it was that came flowing through the Common to them.'

'It is a weakness we shall not have,' asserted a junior officer creech solemnly.

The medical creech smiled at the note of self-assertiveness in the younger creech's voice; he would never have spoken in that tone while Marshal Koli lived. *The young ones*, the medical creech realised, *will adjust and rebuild. But let us hope that they will not turn their thoughts to interplanetary conquest. That mistake has already been made once—and once is sufficient.*

'Let us return home,' the medical creech said, and the others moved off to prepare the huge ship for the return voyage.

Now, thought the medical creech sombrely, *we are responsible for ourselves.*

This odd and novel idea appealed to him, attracted him; yet at the same time it filled him with dread. *Now that we have freedom,* he thought. *I hope it does not prove a burden too great for us.*

17

Gus Swenesgard blinked stupidly at the sudden light.

For a moment his sense of relief was so great that he simply lay there, saying a clumsy prayer to his fundamentalist God, a prayer of thanks; then a wave of panic swept over him. *Am I,* he asked himself, *still alone?*

He lurched from the bed and staggered to the window. Outside, in the evening darkness, he could see the dusty, familiar street, but nobody inhabited it. His terror increased by the second; hastily, he stumbled out into the hotel corridor and shouted, 'Anybody there?'

'I'm here, boss.' The voice of one of his faithful Toms; it resounded from beyond a turn in the corridor. Gus broke into a run in the direction of the sound. 'You're fat and mean,' the Tom said, when they stood facing each other, seeing each other, 'but you're better than nothing.' His voice cracked with emotion.

Gus said, 'You're lazy as an old dog and ugly as a toad. But I never saw a better sight than your face this minute.' Both men exploded into near-hysterical laughter and other voices around them were laughing, too. One of the hotel rooms opened, then another; the occupants streamed shakily out, shouting greetings to one another.

In the centre of the swirling mass of humanity, Gus shouted, 'I'm gonna have all them doors taken off their hinges. This is gonna be the first hotel in the world with no doors!' *They love me*, Gus thought with awe. *They really love me; see how they throw their arms around me. And that old lady just kissed me. It's a miracle of love that's happened. It's God's message of love to all mankind.* 'Hey,' Gus shouted above the hubbub, 'how would you like for me to be king?'

One of the Toms shouted back, 'You can be anything you damn well please, Mr Gus. Just let me look at you!'

Other voices joined in. 'Hooooray for King Gus! Long live King Gus! Gus the King!'

Gus broke away from the crowd and stumped puffingly down the hall to a vidphone. Shaking with excitement, coins sliding from his fingers and bouncing to the floor, he put through a call to the nearest TV network station. 'This is Gus Swenesgard,' he declared. 'I want to buy an hour of prime time on a worldwide satellite hookup for, say, tomorrow night.' He got hold of the station manager, repeated this.

'On whose authority?' the station manager said.

'I'm the acting head of the bale of Tennessee,' Gus said sharply.

'Can you pay for it?' The station manager quoted an approximate price.

Blinking, Gus said, 'S-s-sure.' It would break him financially—but it was worth it.

'You've made yourself a purchase,' the station manager said. 'We might as well put you on the air as anybody else; at least you're human. Since the lights went on all hell's breaking loose around here. You know what's going on now? Our head newscaster is in front of the cameras taking off his clothes and shouting "I love you". In a minute I expect he'll start doing something really crazy, like telling the truth.'

'Then I've got the time slot?' Gus could hardly believe it.

'Sure. But payment has to be in advance of the telecast.'

'Worldwide?'

'You bet your sweet life.'

'Yippy!' Gus shouted.

'Hey,' the station manager said. 'Say "yippy" again. I love to hear a man sound so happy.'

'Yippy!' shouted Gus into the phone.

'Why don't you and the wife come down and have dinner with us before the telecast?' the station manager asked. 'I sure would like my family to meet the acting head of the bale of Tennessee.'

'I don't have any wife,' Gus said. 'You see . . .'

'Well, that's okay. You can marry my eldest girl. I'm sure after what's happened you'd appear pretty good to her no matter how you look.'

'I'll take you up on the dinner part, anyway,' Gus said, and, thanking the man, hung up. *They love me,* he thought again. *Everyone in the world loves me.*

The vidphone rang. Gus, being close to it, answered it.

'Gus Swenesgard?' inquired a voice. The screen remained blank. But sometimes this particular phone did that; he wasn't surprised.

'Yes, this is Gus.' It seemed to him there was something familiar about the voice; he could not, however, place it. And in addition there was something frightfully

180

strange about it, too; the voice raised goose-bumps on Gus' flabby flesh.

'So you want to be king.' The unidentified voice held contempt; cold, pitiless contempt.

'Sure,' Gus answered, suddenly not quite so sure of himself. *Here,* he realised with a sinking feeling, *is at least one person who doesn't love me.*

'I know you, Gus Swenesgard,' the voice declared. 'I know you better than you know yourself. You can't even rule your own gluttony; how do you expect to rule others when you can't rule yourself?'

'I'm no worse than the next . . .' Gus began defensively.

'Is that a reason to call yourself "king"? Just because you're no worse than the next person?' The voice had become hard and ruthless. 'You're a clown, Gus; a redneck, ranting, second-rate clown.' The voice rolled on relentlessly. 'You hypocrite. Egomaniac. Overstuffed racist slob with a rear-end like a hog's snout.'

Frightened, Gus said. 'W-w-who do you think you are, anyhow?'

'Don't you know me?'

'Hell no.' Nobody talked to him that way; at least nobody had for a long time.

'You were present at my birth. Don't you remember? In the great darkness, in the silence.'

'What are you, some kind of nut?' His voice shook.

'You would like to be able to reduce me to the stature of a mere nut, wouldn't you? I know how you think, Gus, how you divide humans into good men and bad men, the saved and the damned. And you, of course, are one of the saved.'

'I'm a good Christian,' Gus muttered, rallying.

'You believe,' the voice continued implacably, 'that

181

the flesh is evil, but you can't escape it. You're helpless to stop the regular, persistent functions of your body, the functions you regard as dirty and sinful and unmentionable, and so you live in constant guilt. You are an abomination, Gus; to me and to everyone—to yourself most of all. You can never be king, Gus; you have a powerful enemy who will sabotage everything you do, everything you try, step by step. As you build it up he will tear it down.'

'Who?' Gus shouted, now thoroughly terrified. 'Who'll do that to me?'

'I will,' the voice said. And the receiver clicked.

Gus, stepping unsteadily away from the dead vidphone, heard the gales of laughter from down the hall; for a moment it seemed to him that the merrymakers were laughing at him, personally. But of course that couldn't be.

Just some crank, he thought shakily. *I mustn't pay him no mind.*

But the words on the phone had gone right through him, like a burning knife, and now they haunted him. Try as he would he couldn't forget them.

I've got work to do, he told himself. And slunk off back to his room, to write his forthcoming TV speech—and finish off the bottle of Cutty Sark.

Joan still sat quietly in the waiting room when Paul Rivers emerged from the general practitioner's office, both hands bandaged and all his fingers in organic splints. 'You didn't have to stay,' he said to her. 'I can manage all right by myself.' *However,* he thought, *I'm glad you did.* In actuality he could *not* manage—and would not for some time. And both of them knew it.

Joan opened the door for him and accompanied him

182

out into the hall. He realised that she had noticed his limp and tried to walk as naturally as possible. *I don't, he reflected, want her to feel sorry for me . . . but that's silly; of course; she feels nothing for me, one way or the other. It's a part of her conditioning that she be indifferent to such matters.*

Still, she had taken the trouble to drag his unconscious body into the ionocraft, give him first aid and bring him here to the doctor. She had not merely left him there in the cave to die, as she easily could have done.

As they stepped into the elevator, Joan said haltingly, 'Paul, I . . .' She then stopped. The elevator door slid shut and they descended in silence. At last she continued, 'It seemed so strange, up there in the mountains. Being you. Yet in another way not so strange being you. As if some part of me—this is how it felt—some part of me had always been you.'

The elevator door opened again, allowing them to exit into the main lobby of the medical building. Paul said, 'I felt the same thing about you, when I became part of you.' They stepped out of the elevator and made their way through the crowd of milling, shouting, happy people, some of whom now and then grabbed and hugged them. Paul did not object to their shoving him about, even though, because of his injuries, the experience was painful. The mob thinned out near the front entrance, and once again he and Joan could hear each other.

'In a way it felt good,' Joan said, 'being you. A real, living, feeling, caring human being. Now, of course, it's too late for me.'

Paul stopped and looked at her intently; her eyes had become moist and in the lights of evening they glistened. *This has got to be an hallucination,* he thought with astonishment. Joan Hiashi crying? Impossible.

183

'I have a problem,' Joan said wistfully; she looked away from him. 'I have nothing and I want nothing; I've achieved the state that holy men have striven for down throughout centuries and now—I want out.'

'Joan,' he said, with an intensity he couldn't conceal. 'Don't you see the contradiction in what you just said? *You do want something.*'

'Something I can never have.' Her voice sagged with hopelessness.

'That's not true.' He touched her shoulder gently with his bandaged right hand. 'Just your wanting to re-enter the world of the shared reality means that the battle is half won. Now, because you want something, I can help you. If you'll let me, of course.'

'You'll teach me?' Her voice had lost a little of its grey overcast of hopelessness.

'I'll teach you how to be with people. And you can teach me how to be alone.'

'Between us,' Joan said wonderingly, 'we have it all. Don't we?' Abruptly she stood on tiptoe to kiss him on the cheek.

Laughing recklessly, Paul trotted out onto the sidewalk, shouting, 'Taxi! Taxi!'

All the taxis had been taken; they had to wait a long time, standing side by side. But that did not bother them; it struck both Joan and Paul as perfectly all right.

Most smells did not bother the not overly-sensitive nostrils of Gus Swenesgard, but for some obscure reason the relatively faint odour of ozone, of electricity, in the TV studio did. *They ought*, he thought with annoyance, *to air this place out once in a while*. But maybe it was just that the prospect ahead of him made him tense.

Everything appeared to be in readiness for the telecast. Gus had personally supervised the installation of the idiot cards from which he would read his prepared speech. And he had, in addition, personally selected the heart-moving, patriotic music which would play softly in the background while he spoke.

He had even personally written the spot announcements that had been telecast at intervals throughout the day, preparing the world for the big moment.

Glancing towards the entrance of the studio Gus saw Dr Paul Rivers just coming in, with Joan Hiashi on his arm. From Dr Rivers' bandaged hands and limping gait Gus gathered that he had met with a major accident, perhaps the result of too much celebrating. Putting on his best political smile Gus waddled over to greet them.

'Hey,' he said fondly, glad to see friends, 'what do you think of the funny smell in here? Or maybe I'm just tense; is that it?' He peered at Paul Rivers nervously, awaiting his professional answer.

'I hadn't noticed anything,' Paul Rivers said genially.

'Well, you don't run a hotel,' Gus said, frowning. 'I wouldn't allow no smell like this in my hotel. Guests might complain.' He had, then, the sudden feeling that Paul Rivers might be silently laughing at him—and glanced suspiciously in the doctor's direction. But Paul seemed perfectly straight-faced. *I must,* Gus thought, *be getting stage-shy.* He mopped his forehead, then; drops of greasy sweat had begun, as always, to stand out on his mottled flesh.

'You're on in five minutes,' said a thin technician with glasses. 'Five minutes, Mr Swenesgard.' The technician hurried busily off.

'Would you like a tranquilliser?' Paul Rivers asked Gus.

'No, no; I'll be okay,' Gus muttered. He wandered nervously off, found his way into the dressing cubicle which the studio people had assigned him and took a good, healthy drag on a bottle of Early Times bourbon. *That,* he told himself with satisfaction, *is the only tranquilliser Gus Swenesgard needs.*

The door opened; Gus hastily hid the bottle behind him. 'Four minutes, Mr Swenesgard,' the technician with the glasses said.

'Go 'way,' grumbled Gus. 'You make me jumpy.'

The technician departed, but Gus knew with grim certainty that he would soon be back to say, 'Three minutes Mr Swenesgard.' So he stumped out of his cubicle and took his place at the modern, large table before the TV cameras.

Behind him hung the old pre-war flag of the United Nations. This would be the first time since the Gany occupation that this flag had been publicly displayed. *A nice touch,* Gus said to himself.

'Three minutes, Mr Swenesgard.'

A weird feeling came over Gus at that moment, an eerie sensation of being watched. *Someone,* he thought, *is staring at me.* He looked around the studio. Yes, a lot of individuals here and there, including Paul Rivers and the Jap girl, had their eyes on him—not to mention the cameramen. But it wasn't that.

I know what it is, he said to himself. *It's the entire people of the world. The whole cottonpickin' planet; that's who's watching me.*

This answer satisfied him intellectually, but emotionally there still remained a nagging feeling of the uncanny, an uneasiness—even fear—that could not rationally be explained.

'Two minutes, Mr Swenesgard.' The thin technician with glasses, hovering.

Now Gus localised the feeling. It emanated from the general direction of the stand on which his idiot cards rested, neatly stacked and waiting.

But there was nobody there, nobody within ten feet of the cards.

'One minute, Mr Swenesgard.'

Gus, suddenly, felt a powerful urge to get to his feet and walk out of the studio, an intuition that to go on would only be to court disaster. However, it had become too late; the cameras had already begun dollying into focus on him, and a ghostly hush had fallen over the studio as the *ON THE AIR* sign became illuminated.

Theres' someone, Gus thought in panic, *or something in this studio, and it's out to get me.*

The announcer started his introduction. Next to the idiot cards stood the technician with the glasses, ready to turn the cards one by one . . . or was it the man with the glasses? Some peculiar variety of blackness had gathered in the area of the cards; one moment Gus could discern the man with the glasses and the next moment he could not.

Gus shook his head, trying to clear his vision, but it appeared to be no use. *What*, he thought quaveringly, *if I can't see the cards?* But, fortunately, the cards themselves seemed to remain clear enough. And as for the intermittent invisibility of the card-turner, well, it was kind of dim in the studio, of course, the bright lights being on so as to confront Gus; they blinded him nearly, making him blink and squint. Perhaps it was just a trick of the lighting.

Now, from beside one of the three cameras, a finger pointed starkly at Gus. He was on!

Staring at the cards like a man hypnotised he began slowly to speak. 'Ladies and gents, good evening, or good morning or afternoon, as the case may be, depending on just where the heck you happen to live on this great, wonderful planet of ours that God has given us, and quite recently given back, thanks to Merciful Providence. I'm your neighbour, Gus Swenesgard, and I run a quiet little bale down here in the southern part of the U.S.A. that you might have heard of in connection with the trouble we've had with Neeg-parts, called Tennessee. I'm just coming on TV like this, informally, to sort of talk to you as neighbour to neighbour about the world situation which, thanks to in some measure my own efforts, we happen to find ourselves plunk in the middle of.'

The chief engineer in the control room glanced at the station manager and they both grinned. Gus, from where he sat, could see them. *What in hell is so funny?* he thought angrily.

'Now,' he continued doggedly, 'that them worms has been chased out and the Neeg-parts cleared out of the hills, we got a big job to do cleaning up the mess that has collected around here during the occupation. Now, you might not think it to look at me, but I . . .

In Paris a bearded café owner reached to turn off his set, which was presenting an instantaneous translation of Gus' speech. 'Merde,' said the Frenchman.

In Rome the Pope changed channels, searching for a good Italian western.

In Kyoto, Japan, a Zen master laughed himself into a fit of hiccups.

In Detroit, Michigan, an ionocraft worker threw a can of beer through the picture tube.

But Gus, not knowing these things, continued. '. . .

now you might think some high-flown military man is the one for the job. But our military failed us, and furthermore . . .'

Something had gone wrong. The speech was not exactly as he had written it. Or was it? *Has someone edited it?* he asked himself. *Or maybe mixed up the cards?*

'The man for the job is someone like me, a clown.'

Gus stopped in mid-sentence and reread the card. That's what it said. 'Clown'.

Now the card was being changed, but Gus could not see the hand which turned it. 'Redneck, ranting, second-rate demagogue,' the next card read. The card turned again. 'Hypocrite, egomaniac, overstuffed racist slob,' the card said.

My God, Gus thought. *That's what the voice on the vidphone called me.*

Hardly knowing what he did he sprang to his feet and shouted, 'You there by the cards; who are you? What's the matter with you?'

The blackness swept towards him, billowing in his direction like an evil wind, and a voice, the same voice which he had heard over the vidphone, said, 'I am your interior self, liberated by my disgust for you and all that you stand for, struck off by the great darkness. I stand outside of space-time, and I judge you.' The darkness surrounded Gus, then, and he found himself back in the occult and hideous condition he had been in so recently, bodiless in the empty silence, the utter blackness, alone with the fading after-image of his own reflection in the cracked, yellowing mirror. Of the hotel room.

He screamed but could not hear the sound of his scream.

Paul Rivers, however, could hear it.

And so could the staff of the TV station.

So could the world, or rather that miniscule portion of it that still continued to listen to Gus' fiasco.

The producer cut Gus off the air and ran the only item he had ready, a commercial for a popular brand of marihuana cigarettes, filter-tip Berkely Boo, 'A little stick of California Sunshine.'

Paul sprang to his feet and limped to Gus' side, ready to give what aid he could; he had seen the hazy black vortex flying at Gus, engulfing him and then disappearing as suddenly as it had appeared.

I'll bet, Paul thought as he remembered the effects he had already seen resulting from the use of Balkani's illusion projectors, *that the phenomenon is some kind of after-effect of the hell-weapon.* 'What is it?' he asked Gus, placing a steadying arm around the bulbous little man's shoulders.

'Are you a doctor?' Gus mumbled, blinking dazedly.

'That's right,' Paul said, aware that Gus could barely see him. 'Leave everything to me,' he said, helping Gus to walk from the illuminated area before the cameras— and from Gus' hoped-for political and military power.

In the lounge Dr Choate and Ed Newkom waited. Seeing them, Gus said quaveringly, 'H-h-how did I do tonight?'

The truth, Paul thought, *will hurt vividly. But you'd never believe a lie.* 'You were awful,' Paul said to Gus Swenesgard. 'The feedback systems register as follows: by the time you left the air only a handful of people, mostly from your own bale, were still watching. Though when you started you had the largest audience any one man has had in the entire history of television.'

Gus said to him, 'You understand about psychology, don't you, sir?'

'If anyone does,' Ed Newkom said, 'Paul does.'

'Can you help me?' Gus asked, studying Paul's face anxiously. 'Can you write speeches for me that'll make people change their minds and listen? Can you tell me what to do to get them back?'

Dr Choate said, 'Yes, as a matter of fact we were planning to offer you our collective professional services in that capacity.'

Paul, too, looked at Gus with admiration. *You fall,* he realised, *but in a moment you're up again, ready to try something else, ready to face the bitter pill of your mistakes. Never willing to give up. And the World Psychiatric Association will be only too glad to take control of your campaign . . . keeping you on as a figurehead, though of course you will always imagine that you are running things. We're wise enough to offer you that. And we will be the strongest political force available in this disorganised reconstruction period—possibly strong enough to make you king after all, at least until normal democratic institutions can be set in motion again.*

Now Gus Swenesgard had recovered his poise and had begun excitedly talking to Dr Choate, planning, scheming, plotting, wildly guessing at the future, while Dr Choate and Ed Newkom nodded, each with a professional medical smile, secure in the knowledge of where the real power lay.

Paul felt admiration for Gus at last, but then he turned and took a good look, perhaps for the first time, at Dr Choate. Did he imagine it, or was there a certain calculating hardness in Dr Choate's eyes?

191

Shaking himself, Paul forced in place the same professional smile visible on the faces of his two colleagues. And thought, *If we can't trust ourselves, who can we trust?*

It seemed to him a good question. But unfortunately —at the moment—he could not readily think of an equally good answer.

If you would like a complete list of Arrow books please send a postcard to
P.O. Box 29, Douglas, Isle of Man, Great Britain.